Highland Vow

Also by J.L. Jarvis

Lydia's Pine Harbor Christmas

Holiday House
The Christmas Cabin
The Winter Lodge
The Lighthouse
The Christmas Castle
The Beach House
The Christmas Tree Inn
The Holiday Hideaway

Highland Passage
Highland Passage
Knight Errant
Lost Bride

Highland Soldiers
The Enemy
The Betrayal
The Return
The Wanderer

American Hearts
Secret Hearts
Forbidden Hearts
Runaway Hearts

For more information, visit jljarvis.com.

Get monthly book news at news.jljarvis.com.

Highland Vow

J.L. Jarvis

BOOKBINDER PRESS

HIGHLAND VOW

ISBN (paperback) 978-1-942767-36-7
ISBN (ebook) 978-1-942767-14-5

Published by Bookbinder Press
bookbinderpress.com

Chapter One

Scotland, 1742

It wasn't just land. It was Scotland, and Gowan was home. Still feeling the sway of the ship underfoot, Gowan stepped onto firm Scottish ground, then he and his fellow soldiers made their way to the nearest dockside tavern.

He planted himself on a stool at the end of the bar, where he found quiet amusement with a bottle nearby and a view of his friends shaking off the memories of war with drink, women, and laughter. A pretty young woman with fiery hair appeared at Gowan's side and draped her arms over his shoulders.

With a warm smile and a wink, he said, "Not tonight, lass."

Weary and troubled by what lay ahead, Gowan wanted to be on his own for the evening to wallow in grief, undisturbed. Weeks had passed since his best friend had died in battle, but coming home brought a fresh release of emotion he hadn't expected. In time, he would find peace with his grief, but for now, he would live with the weight of regret.

Gowan ate as fine a meal as he'd had in months, which said more for the hardships he'd endured than the innkeeper's cook, then he ascended the stairs to the room he'd secured. After lying awake for more than an hour, at last, he found solace in sleep.

Dew clung to the grass in heavy droplets as Gowan emerged from the tavern the following morning. He headed straight for the stables and found a fine beast in need of a new owner and an owner in want of Gowan's coin. He paid more than the horse was worth, but he rode away atop the gelding, feeling like the master of his own destiny for the first time in years. As he rode, he reached over and touched the sgian-achlais under his left arm. The blade had belonged to his friend Robert Innes, who wouldn't need it anymore.

By midmorning, Gowan was well on his way down an old drovers' road with the faint sun on his back. In good weather, the trip took an hour, but this was not good weather. There were mists, then there were Scots mists— the sort a man could practically reach out and hold in his hand. This was a proper Scots mist, and he thanked God he was back home to feel it.

His ship had gone off course in a storm, and they'd pulled into the nearest harbor, far short of Inverness, as had been the plan. Any harbor would have done rather than face any more of the storm's fury, so he had no complaint except one—he could not see his own hands before him, let alone the road. But through gaps in the mist now and then, he caught glimpses of road beaten down by the hooves of cattle and horses that had trodden the path over the years. He gave his horse a pat on the neck. At least one of them seemed to know the way, and for that, Gowan was grateful.

It was not his own home he sought. He'd lost that, or what was left of it, before he left.

When the laird's son threatened his family, his father fought back and lost. The sun had risen and burned through the clouds as Gowan held his lifeless father and cursed the laird and his men. His mother had soon followed her husband, leaving Gowan alone with his grief.

He'd buried his parents and left with one goal in mind. He would go off to war and fight as a mercenary with all the rage that burned in his soul. Beyond that, he made no plans, for to do so required hope for the future, and he had none. He expected no more from life than to die in battle. But instead, he had lived, and he would do so alone, for he would not wish his life on a family.

Having reconciled himself to the life before him, Gowan carried the key to his future. The letter of introduction in his sporran promised to secure him a place, if not forever, then temporarily. It was a chance to find a new home, but it was not without cost. He had made a promise—a solemn vow, Robert had called it. He had made Gowan take an oath on his dirk that he would look after Robert's sister, Morna.

Their mother had died giving birth to her, and Morna had suffered the blame for that death. She was never abused or neglected but was simply left feeling unloved by anyone except Robert.

Gowan had no delusions of what his place would be at Robert's home. The best he could hope for would be for the laird to grant him a position in his castle guard.

From there, Gowan would be able to keep an eye on Morna. How hard could it be to offer kindness now and then or a dance when he saw the poor wallflower alone at a ceilidh. From what Robert told him about her, such kindness would be easy. She had always been a reticent girl who spent too much time alone but without complaint. Looking after her would be no harder than having a sister, something he'd never had. With no family of his own, he looked forward to it.

Through the mist came the sound of water tripping over stones. His horse needed little urging to draw closer to drink. In the gaps in the mist, Gowan caught sight of a meandering brook that fed into a small pool. He dismounted to lead his horse to it. While his horse drank, Gowan took a few steps away and relieved himself. As he stood there, he spied something light at the edge of the water. When he was finished, he walked over, knelt down on one knee, and picked up the folded cloth to examine it. Roughly woven and well worn, it was the typical garb of a crofter. He looked up, clothing still wadded in his hand. When he could not find anyone, alarm seized him. *Is the person who shed these clothes drowning? Or worse, has it already happened?* He started to take a step forward but was stopped by a cold metal blade pressed against his neck.

Chapter Two

Gowan cursed his folly at letting his guard down. *Have I survived war only to return home and meet my demise at the hands of a bloody bandit?*

He lowered his eyes and caught a sideways look at the arm holding the blade. With a hand so small and smooth, he could be no more than a lad.

Gowan watched the hand, for it was all he could see to judge any reaction. "I've naught but a few coins, but they're yours if you'll kindly remove that knife from my neck." By the time he had finished the sentence, he had flipped the boy over and was rewarded with a well-deserved grunt as the wind was knocked out of him... *her*.

She covered her naked body as well as she could with her hands while Gowan came to his senses. When he realized he was holding her clothes in his hand, he tossed her the bundle. While she scrambled to get dressed, he managed to retrieve the dirk she had dropped when she fell. With that safely stowed in his belt, he stood, arms folded, while she finished scrambling to clothe herself and stand up to face him.

Other than having pressed her knife to his neck, she posed little threat now, so he thought they might come to some sort of agreement—one that did not involve stabbing or robbing. "Look, lass, I'm willing to overlook your assault—"

She threw herself at him and knocked him to the ground.

"My God!" He rolled on top of her and pinned her wrists to the ground. "Och! You're a wee bit high-strung." He struggled to keep her from lashing out at him again.

Suddenly, she stopped and looked straight at him. She was no match for his strength, and something in her eyes told him she knew it. He could almost see her thinking and planning her next move. When he'd thoroughly immobilized her, she averted her eyes, clenching her jaw. She appeared to be bracing herself.

When he realized for what, the thought shocked him. Gowan said, "Whatever you might think, I'm not going to hurt you."

She cast a harsh glare at him as though he were her enemy, when she was the one who had attacked him. Yet in her present predicament, he could hardly blame her for her apparent mistrust. There she lay, pinned beneath a strange man.

Seeing what she must have thought was hesitation, she began squirming beneath him to free herself. He watched her in disbelief. *Does she really think she can prevail in this struggle?* She lifted her eyes, which were full of fear and mistrust. For a moment, Gowan lost himself in those lovely brown pools. His eyes swept over her face and her hair, which were both smooth as silk. He was suddenly moved to kiss her.

Gowan abruptly stood up and helped her to her feet while he kept a firm grasp on her wrists. He studied her face, which had softened. Clearly, she realized that since he had not attacked her, pursuing her hopeless assault on him would not end to her advantage. Gowan exhaled.

The young woman thrust a knee into his groin.

"Oof!" While he bent over and his hands went to the source of the pain, she punched him in the jaw. Gowan clamped his hand on her wrist before she could withdraw it, then he flipped her around so her back faced him. He circled his other arm around her waist while she clawed and scratched his forearm.

"Good God, lass. I'm trying not to hurt you, but you dinnae make it easy." Annoyed more than angry, he finally managed to immobilize her... again. At last, she seemed to have surrendered the fight.

While he was still holding her from behind, his lips brushed her hair, and his train of thought escaped him. The next moment, he said, "Can we talk about this?"

She scoffed. "Talk?"

Gowan frowned in disbelief. "Aye! To begin with, you stuck a blade into my neck, so you ought to be grateful."

"Grateful?"

From the bitter tone of her voice, he surmised she was not. He looked up to the heavens and sighed. He had no further interest in sparring with her, so he said plainly, "Anyone else would have killed you by now."

"Not if I killed them first."

"Great God, must you be so combative? I'll not harm you unless you force me to it."

"Oh, aye, and how might I do that? By living and breathing, no doubt." Her words were bold, but he could feel her heart pounding. He loosened his grip and turned her around to face him.

Gowan leveled a steady gaze. "Stabbing at me with knives tends to make me a bit crabbit. I'll not be sorry for defending myself from your assault."

She lifted her chin. "You're on Innes land, so I had every right."

"You're an Innes?" That meant he was close to Robert's home.

But before he could inquire further, she bristled. "Aye, and I have but to scream, and you'll have the whole Innes clan here to answer to."

Yet she had not called for assistance, which weakened her claim. Not that he blamed her for lying. Despite his assurances, she clearly felt threatened yet put up a bold front. Gowan's eyes lit as he suppressed a smile.

Fire flared in her eyes. "You find that amusing?"

He forced his eyebrows together and tried to look serious. "No, not at all."

She narrowed her eyes. "Aye, well, I suggest you laugh your way off Innes land before anyone finds us—you—here."

"In truth, I'm bound for Innes House. Can you point me in that direction?"

Annoyance replaced her apprehension. "Why should I?"

Gowan sighed. "Because I'm asking?"

"You might have tried asking before you pinned me to the ground!" Her glaring brown eyes did more damage than that dirk of hers could ever manage at her hand.

"In self-defense."

"You might have caused serious bodily harm."

"Lass, if I'd wanted to harm you, I'd have done it by now."

"Dinnae 'lass' me."

Gowan ran his fingers through his wavy dark hair. "Och. You are a disagreeable *lass*."

"Only with your sort." She scowled.

"Oh, my sort, is it? And what sort is that?" He shrugged in disbelief and took a step back, shaking his head.

"The sort who throws ladies on the ground then pins them there with their filthy paws."

Now that was uncalled for. He looked down and turned his hands over. Well, there might be some truth to her words. "Aye, well, it so happens that I was about to rinse off my hands in that stream when you poked your dirk at my neck, so the state of my hands is your fault, not mine. Which reminds me, what were you thinking—attacking a man a head taller than you? Not that I'm one to boast, but a wee lass like yourself stands no chance against me."

"Just because something seems impossible doesnae mean you shouldnae try." Her nostrils were flaring, which was not her best look.

"Charming. When you get home, be sure and stitch that up on a needlework sampler."

Her eyes flared. He seemed to have touched a raw nerve. Despite taking a bit of pleasure from that, Gowan had had enough social discourse. He turned to retrieve his horse and be on his way when she landed a punch to his kidney. With a grunt of pain, he grabbed hold of her wrist and looked skyward. He'd gone to war, trained hard off the field between battles, and there he was, being pummeled by a wee lass. It was his fault for underestimating her.

While he contemplated where their little encounter had gone so horribly wrong, she said, "I hate needlework."

"I'll be sure to remember that."

"And I attacked you because you took my clothes, and I couldnae go home without them."

He cocked his head to the side, which was as close as he was inclined to go toward admitting that she'd made a good point.

She appeared to have finished making her point, so Gowan said, "I did have your clothes, so I can understand how you might have felt the need to take action. I dinnae expect you to believe me, but when I came upon them, I feared that you'd drowned. I was trying to help you."

She lifted her chin as her eyebrows drew together.

He took that as a concession. "I am willing to overlook your assault on my person and release you—provided you promise to leave me alone."

He waited, but she did not reply.

"For God's sake, lass, what more do you want? I'd have hurt you by now if I'd been so inclined." He lowered his voice. "But I'm not. You have my word."

Although she was silent, she hadn't kicked, punched, or scratched. That was progress. He could not resist an admiring smile. "You put up a good fight—"

Her eyes lit as she practically smiled.

Then he finished the thought. "For a lass."

She slapped him in the face. "So do you."

Now what? Can she not take a compliment? He shrugged. There was no understanding some people.

She narrowed her eyes then put two fingers in her mouth and whistled. A horse emerged from the woods.

He couldn't help but admire her. She had more combat skill than any lass he'd known—and some lads—and she'd trained her horse well. But it wasn't her skill that intrigued him at the moment. A curving plait of hair languidly draped over her shoulder had fallen to reveal a bare, satin-skinned path from her neck to her shoulder. He resisted an impulse to reach out to touch it.

She gave her horse a pat on the neck and prepared to mount it and ride off. It would have been a spectacular exit had she been able to accomplish it. Instead, she groaned in pain, leaned on the horse for a moment, tried again, then cursed.

"Are you hurt?" Without thinking, he stretched his fingers out to touch her.

She turned around to face him with eyes filled with fury. What a beauty she was, even in anger. "It's my back."

Her pained expression softened his heart. "May I help you?"

The girl drew her eyebrows together as she averted her gaze. It must have killed her to say it. "If you would. Please."

"You'll not stab me, will you?"

"Och! You're impossibly vexing."

Gowan began to reach out then withdrew his hand. "I must wash my hands first. I've been told that they're filthy."

She scoffed and grabbed hold of his shoulder.

He tilted his head. "Although you're the one doing

most of the touching. Not that I blame you for not being able to keep your hands off me, but still..."

Before she could react, Gowan hoisted her into the saddle. He folded his arms and enjoyed her reaction. It was practically worth the inconvenience of the earlier knife to the neck and subsequent blows just to watch and lay odds as to when steam would come out of her ears.

"Good day, sir." She turned abruptly and rode off.

"Was it something I said?" Gowan watched as she rode away. "Lovely lass. 'Tis a shame she's so shy."

Chapter Three

The midmorning sun burned off the fog to reveal a castle, just as Robert had described it. It had to be Innes House. After presenting his letter of introduction as proof to the guards that he was, indeed, bringing word of the laird's son, Robert Innes, they opened the gate. He was taken to the parlor and left alone there with the laird. When Malcolm Innes turned from the window to greet him, the sight took Gowan by surprise. The same eyes he had come to know well now looked back into his with the sort of calm bearing only a powerful man could afford. That formidable stance and broad shoulders had served his son well to the end.

"Forgive me, sir, but the resemblance caught me off guard."

"Aye?" He peered at Gowan with assessing eyes.

"Robert and I fought side by side in the war of Austrian Succession." Gowan paused, knowing news of his son's fate could not have reached the laird yet.

The fixed gaze that met his held the inevitable conclusion of what Gowan's visit must mean for his son, and the light faded from Malcolm's eyes. "You fought beside Robert. Yet you've come here alone."

"Aye, sir. I'm sorry. I bring sad news... of Robert." As much as he had imagined this moment, he still stumbled over the words. He handed Robert's sgian-achlais to Malcolm.

Malcolm stared at the knife. "I gave this to him when he was a lad." He ran his thumb over the worn and stained leather-bound dirk handle that bore the Clan Innes crest. He took a breath and said curtly, "So he's gone, then." His expression hardened as he lifted cold eyes to meet Gowan's. "How do I ken you didnae just take this from his dead body in battle?"

"He said you would say that." Gowan held the man's gaze as he handed him the letter. "He wrote this in case anything happened. And he told me to tell you that the bearer of this blade spoke the truth just as surely as Robert always had done—including the time he told you about the lass in the village."

Malcolm cast a sharp look at Gowan.

Gowan hastened to add, "I only repeat what he said to relay to you." Robert had warned him to expect a reaction.

Robert explained that he had fallen in love too early and too well, but his father had not believed it was love. He was too young for such nonsense. Besides, his father had other plans for his son, and they did not include marrying an ordinary girl from the village. He was only fifteen at the time, and his father insisted that first love was fleeting. But this love lasted. Robert and Briana met in secret over the next few years, hoping, in time, Malcolm would soften. But when an arranged betrothal to someone Malcolm considered more suitable was announced, father and son exchanged words. Only then did Malcolm tell him he'd paid the family what for them must have been a king's ransom to move to a faraway croft somewhere in the Highlands. Briana was gone. Had she and her family not left, Malcolm would have turned them out. Robert could not blame her. She'd had no choice but to break his heart. With the only woman he would ever love now lost to him, Robert bade a bitter farewell to his father and went away to fight in any war that would have him.

Frowning, Malcolm said, "Aye, I remember, as he knew I would." He lowered his eyes and swallowed. When he looked up, whatever dark memory Gowan had invoked was gone, leaving only the grief of a father for his only son.

Gowan saw the man struggle to choke back his grief. He needed time alone. "If you'll excuse me, I'm sure you've matters to attend to."

Abstractedly, Malcolm said, "Aye."

Gowan went to the door, where the guard who had escorted him still waited.

Malcolm said to the guard, "Have cook prepare Mr. Dunbar something to eat, then tell the servants to prepare Robert's room for him."

Gowan's eyes darted toward Malcolm, but he quickly looked downward.

Malcolm said, "'Tis only four walls and a floor. I'm sure Robert wouldnae have minded."

"N-No, sir, but I-I thank you," Gowan stammered,

surprised by the unexpected generosity. But the moment passed quickly.

Of course Robert wouldn't have minded. Gowan had saved his life twice, and Robert had been there for him in turn. But Robert had continued to seek ways to repay him, even though Gowan begged him to stop every time. Friends, which they had been from the start, should never have scores to settle. They would watch out for each other in battle, and when it was over, they would have no debts to pay. They'd agreed that was how it would be.

So Gowan thanked Malcolm for his kind hospitality then turned and followed the servant to Robert's room. Once inside and alone, Gowan sat on the edge of the bed. He stared blankly at the sumptuous decorations that filled the room. Dark and imposing furniture seem to anchor the room with its presence, softened only by richly hued tapestries. From the two corner windows, sun bathed the room in light.

Gowan had never known comfort like it. It grieved him to be there in Robert's stead. If he'd only turned one second sooner, he might have saved Robert's life. But he hadn't. Gowan had been fighting another soldier and finished him off too late to help Robert. By the time Gowan had turned, it was done.

He surrendered to exhaustion and lay back on the bed, staring at the canopy overhead. The same thought that had kept him awake many nights troubled him now.

It should have been me.

Two Months Earlier

Swords clashed, and men cursed and called out. Enemy soldiers were upon them, and they fought them off valiantly.

Then came the moment Gowan would relive again and again in the weeks that would follow. But no matter how many times he went through every step of it, the outcome was the same.

Gowan ran his sword through a soldier, pulled it out, and turned just as Robert was struck from behind. Gowan didn't even have time to warn him. Robert looked down, saw the tip of the sword in his chest, then looked up at Gowan. Their eyes met as Gowan finished off Robert's attacker. When the enemy soldier continued to breathe, Gowan grabbed his dirk and sliced the man's throat. Robert slumped to the ground, but before Gowan could attend to his friend, another soldier came at him. Time slowed. All he thought of was finishing the enemy off. And when no one was left to fight, he rushed to Robert, who needed a doctor, and Gowan would find him. Nothing else mattered. But Robert gripped Gowan's arm and managed a weak "No."

Gowan protested even as he saw how hopeless it was. But he had to do something. If he could only get Robert to a doctor, his friend would survive.

Robert's eyes shone as if he might be trying to smile. "God, you're a stubborn bastard. Just let me go."

Although Gowan shook his head, he knew Robert was right. He gripped Robert's hand as if his grip might keep him from passing to the other side. Robert started to talk, but his voice was too faint. Gowan bent down. Robert reached a weak hand toward his pocket, and Gowan helped him retrieve an envelope.

"Read it." But before Gowan could, Robert said, "Will you look after Morna?"

Gowan nodded. They'd talked about all of that before, what they'd do if one of them died in battle. But at that moment, if Robert had asked him to capture the moon, he would have agreed.

Each breath came with increasing difficulty as Robert continued. "I promised her I'd come home. She needs me, and I've failed her." He looked up at Gowan. "Take the letter. My father will give you a home there. Promise. Swear to me you'll..." He kept trying to speak, but no words would come out.

"I promise." He tightened his grip on Robert's hand. "Do you hear me? I swear it."

A LOUD KNOCK at Gowan's chamber door woke him abruptly. "Aye?" he called out as he sat up and raked his fingers through his hair.

A boy's voice answered. "I was sent to bring you down to supper."

His eyebrows drew together, and he slowly nodded. "One moment."

He went to the washbasin and splashed water on his face. As he dried it, he looked out the window. A gentle breeze brushed the grasses as the sun shone on what was left of the day. He had missed the wild hills that reached up toward the heavens. Deceptively smooth from afar, those dark-green slopes could be cruel to anyone who dared travel upon them. But he had grown up on the other side of those hills. He knew every inch of that brutal terrain, and he loved it.

It was good to be back, but it brought him little peace or contentment. He'd expected to feel different. But how could it be the same with no family or home to return to? The haunting beauty was but a reminder of sorrowful times. Gowan shook off his dark mood. He'd been given a gift. That was what he would dwell on.

At some point between battles, Robert had written a letter of introduction to his father, asking him to give Gowan a position as a guard. Gowan understood he would have to pledge his fealty to Clan Innes, but he owed no loyalty anywhere else, so he accepted the condition. With that done, he would be part of the clan. With it came a home and a sense of belonging. In exchange, he would fulfill his promise to look after Robert's sister. It was more than a promise given to ease a dying man's mind. To Gowan, it was a solemn vow that he was determined to fulfill or die trying.

Chapter Four

Gowan walked into the great hall to find everyone seated and beginning to eat. A hush fell as everyone watched him approach the dais and bow to the laird. "My apologies. I'm afraid I overslept."

Malcolm looked at him, unconcerned. "Dinnae fash, lad. You've had a long journey."

The hum of conversation resumed. Malcolm stretched out his arm toward an empty chair on the dais then turned to continue his conversation with the man at his side.

Servants bustled about, setting down platters and pouring ale and wine for Gowan as he sat down. He'd been given the honor of sitting two seats down from the laird, with one empty seat between them.

Gowan barely had time to wonder whose seat it might be when a swish of skirts signaled the hurried arrival of a young lady. She slipped into the empty chair and sat perfectly still, her eyes straight ahead, hands in her lap. With a sharp intake of breath, Gowan realized he had seen her before. She was cleaned up and changed from her earlier peasant garb into fine clothing, but there was no mistaking the woman who had given him a fair beating. Perhaps sensing his steady gaze, she glanced sideways at him. She was surprised, as well, to see the man whose neck she'd held a knife to mere hours before. Her eyes widened in a pleading expression.

His mouth turned up at the corners. Having been the victim of her wrath, he couldn't resist taking a moment to savor her apprehension. "Good evening, my lady."

She maintained an expression of almost perfect poise, so perfect it must have been practiced for years. Only her soft brown eyes gave away secret panic. As she parted her lips to speak, Malcolm turned and interrupted. "Morna, have you met our guest?"

Morna choked then coughed and looked back at Gowan, her eyes bright with fear. She was solely at his mercy, yet her distress unexpectedly moved him.

Gowan smiled at the laird and spoke for her. "We've not had the pleasure."

Malcolm nodded. "Forgive me. Had my daughter been on time, we might have managed a proper introduction before now."

Morna regained her composure except for a muscle that twitched in her jaw.

Gowan bowed his head. "Miss Innes." He lifted earnest eyes to meet hers. After everyone else had resumed conversation with others, Gowan quietly said, "I'm truly sorry to have brought such sad news of your brother. He fought bravely and well, and he spoke of you often."

Her eyes softened as she began to reply, but before she

could speak, Malcolm again interrupted. "Morna is soon to be wed. Are you not, lass?"

Her eyes flitted toward the laird as she said a quick "Aye," then she stared down at her plate.

Malcolm's comment seemed a bit forced, coming as it had while Gowan's eyes had been locked upon Morna's. It seemed almost as if Malcolm felt the need to mark Morna as being unavailable to him, which was a bit heavy-handed, given that they'd only just met, but then he recalled the circumstances under which Robert had left. Perhaps the laird was determined to avoid a similar situation with Morna.

Robert could not deny that Morna was lovely to look at, with flecks of gold in her soft eyes—brown like her brother's. Her hair was not Robert's dark blond but a deep sable that shone when flickers of candlelight caught it. Although it was swept up into a knot, he remembered that same hair tumbling down in a mass of disarrayed strands over her shoulders after he'd thrown her to the ground. Ah yes, he reminded himself, that demure creature knew how to wield a blade.

Gowan realized he was staring and tried to recover. "I wish you and your betrothed many long years of happiness."

With a slight turn to her head, just enough to conceal her expression from her father, she cast a dark look into Gowan's eyes. He wasn't quite sure what it meant, but it had a sharp edge that he guessed was annoyance, at best, or more likely pure anger.

Malcolm grinned. "There's a good lass. Now, dinnae tire Mr. Dunbar with your talk of the wedding."

"No, Father, I promise I will not." She returned her

gaze to the table, and the laird turned away and resumed laughing and talking with what was clearly the preferred side of the table.

"Miss Innes—"

"Please, Mr. Dunbar." She glanced about then lowered her voice. "Let us not make this worse. While I thank you for your discretion, there's no need to force conversation. I've lost a brother. That's enough torment for one evening." She turned away before Gowan could reply.

Realizing he was still staring, Gowan looked down then glanced at his other side, where a young clansman was working very hard to impress the young lady beside him. Morna had to have known he'd have no one else to talk to, but she apparently felt no obligation to make her guest feel at home. But then, he wasn't her guest. He was the laird's, and only out of respect for his son.

Gowan ate his supper and drank his ale in awkward silence. Everywhere his eyes settled, people talked and laughed, all delightfully engaged in the simple enjoyment of others—all but Gowan and Morna.

Morna. He chuckled silently. *Could it be that she has a secret twin tucked away?* The young woman at the table could not be the same woman he'd met hours ago. That woman had been strong and self-assured, which were traits Gowan found appealing enough in women, provided they weren't accompanied by sharp objects. Nor could she be the young woman her brother had described. Her kindness and grace had not leapt out at him yet, but perhaps she feared overwhelming him with her well-concealed charm. No... that would require at least minimal thought about Gowan's well-being. He tried not to laugh.

One moment, she appeared poised and confident, and the next, she was silent to the point of sullenness. In both incarnations, her actions demonstrated a marked lack of the warmth and ease her brother had possessed. He could understand her initial displeasure at the nature of their first meeting, but now there was no such excuse. He might have been raised in a croft, but he knew something of manners.

Then Gowan remembered. In her defense, she was grieving. He'd had time to live with the loss of his friend. It weighed on him still, but his grief no longer showed on the outside. But the news was still fresh to Robert's sister. When Gowan's parents died, he'd retreated even from those who best knew him. Had he met a stranger in the following days, he would have had nothing to offer—not even the simplest conversation. Morna was in such a state. Gowan suddenly felt like a callous blackguard.

He paused from his self-loathing to notice the sumptuous surroundings. Robert had described this place to him. Fine tapestries hung on the walls along with antlers and armaments scattered between. A massive fireplace warmed the hall filled with good spirits and lively conversation. It was no wonder Robert had such fond memories of being there with his loved ones.

Supper was a feast, and the woman beside him was a feast for the eyes in her beautiful dress. Surrounded by family and wealth, she wanted for nothing. While the circumstances of her birth were indeed tragic, losing both mother and, in a sense, her father as well, one would be hard pressed to feel sorry for her life after that. She had grown up in wealth with her every need met. She had never been cruelly ill treated. From what Robert had told him, the laird had done no worse than to busy himself with affairs of the castle and clan.

The surrounding crofts must have been filled with dozens of Highlander children who would have loved to grow up in such surroundings. If this wasn't good enough for Robert's sister, she needed to wake up and look about at the world outside their estate. She'd had far better fortune than most. Yet Gowan wondered why Robert would have implored him to look after Morna.

Regardless of the reason, Gowan was willing. But what he could do for a woman who, grieving or not, refused to make even polite conversation was a mystery to him. He might have helped the woman he'd met earlier, but the only sign of spirit in the woman beside him was the resolute gaze in her downcast eyes. In the span of a few hours, she seemed to have given up caring about others around her, perhaps even herself. So deep was her grief.

He had never promised to converse or comprehend. He had only promised to look after her, and that he would do. While he did not know her exact age, he knew she was slightly younger than Robert, which put her well within marrying age. So marriage in her near future made perfect sense. After he felt confident she would be well cared for, Gowan would watch her walk down the aisle into a life apart from whatever problem had so troubled Robert.

On that day, her husband could have her.

Chapter Five

Morna leaned on the window ledge and looked out at the stars and the gentle moonlit slope of wild grass that led from Innes House to the glen. How they used to run and play on that lawn when they were children. Robert would be the brave warrior and she the enemy soldier. She'd run him through with a wooden blade, and he'd fall. They didn't know they'd been rehearsing his fate.

A swell of emotion overwhelmed her from without and within. She had to get out of this prison and feel the same grass underfoot that she'd felt as a child. She would go to that place where they used to play, and she would weep and cry out where no one would witness the depth of her sorrow. There she would say her farewell to her brother.

WITH AN EXASPERATED SIGH, Gowan got up from his bed and went to the window. He had hoped coming home would bring an end to the sleepless nights he had suffered at war, but he was mistaken. He leaned against the stone window frame and stared into the night. The moon's silver light cast a soft glow on the rolling hills that stretched down to the glen. A movement below caught his eye. There was no mistaking the fact that the flutter of fabric belonged to a woman's cloak. But she was no ordinary woman. The silken sheen of the skirts that peeked out underneath it were too fine for any woman he'd seen there, save one.

With a groan, Gowan muttered, "Morna. Och, lass, what in God's name are you doing now?" His eyebrows furrowed as he shook his head, wishing he had never seen her. But he had.

He quickly wrapped and belted his plaid about his waist, grabbed his sword and dirk, and headed down the spiral stone stairs. Minutes later, he had nearly caught up with her when she turned and spied him in pursuit and lost her footing. She tumbled down the hill. Gowan caught up and stood looking down at her, fists on his hips.

She scrambled halfway to her feet and started to run, but Gowan hooked an arm about her waist and scooped her up to her feet. He held her against him while she flailed her limbs about. He winced as she landed a couple of blows, but he patiently kept her clamped against him until she grew weary and heaved a sigh of frustration.

Gowan loosened his grip enough to turn her around to face him, but he kept her arm firmly in his grip.

She glared at him. "Why won't you leave me alone?"

"Because I dinnae want to watch you—or anyone else —wander off and get lost in those wild hills. People have died doing that. I'd prefer you didn't join them."

She busily smoothed out her skirts. "Thank you, but I can take care of myself."

"You may think that you can."

Straightening, she looked him in the eye. "Because I'd be right. I grew up here, and I know those hills as well as I know my own castle courtyard."

Gowan smiled patiently. "Not well enough to go frolicking about in the moonlight."

Morna frowned. "You dinnae ken what you're talking about."

"I know enough to recognize a young woman too confident for her own good." Gowan's patience was waning.

Her eyes widened as she took in a quick breath. "Thank you, Mr. Dunbar, for your opinion. Now, if you'll excuse me." She turned away, but Gowan touched her arm. She yanked it away and started walking, but Gowan grasped her arm, this time more firmly.

"Miss, I'm sorry, but in good conscience, I cannae let you do this."

She aimed her fiery gaze at him. "Yet in good conscience you feel perfectly comfortable manhandling me."

His voice softened. "I'm sorry for that. But I'll not apologize for trying to protect to you."

Morna rolled her eyes. "Protect me? Please, God, save me from my protectors!" She exhaled. "Mr. Dunbar, consider me rescued. Now please return to your chamber, and let your conscience be troubled no further." She attempted a smile, but the fury in her eyes negated its effect.

Giving her arm a tug, he took a step toward the castle. "God deliver me, woman! You dinnae make it easy."

"What's easy for you is of little concern to me."

Gowan realized he was smiling. Morna was a fine-looking woman, but with fire in her eyes, she was striking. Which was fitting, since the next moment, she struck his cheek with the palm of her hand. He turned his cheek, impressed by the force this lovely lady could muster and by the accompanying sting. He turned back with wide-open eyes and started to speak, but she punched him in the gut. He'd have cursed her if he hadn't been trying to refill his lungs.

Horses' hooves sounded. Morna cried out to two men approaching on horseback. "Thank God you've arrived! This man won't leave me alone. Would you please do something with him?"

"I beg your pardon?" Gowan shot a look at Morna as two castle guards dismounted and seized him.

The older guard said, "What would you like us to do with him?"

Morna's eyes settled on Gowan's then flicked away toward the guards. "I dinnae care. I just want him to leave me alone."

"Aye, madam. We'll make sure you're not bothered again."

Gowan had had enough. "What? You cannae be serious! I was rescuing her." He looked at Morna, pleading for the truth. He thought he saw a moment of panic flash over her face, but it didn't stop her from nodding to the guards. "Thank you."

The older guard turned to the younger. "You take that

rogue to the dungeon, and I'll escort Miss Innes to her chamber."

That caught Morna off guard. "But I didn't mean—I dinnae need an escort."

"'Tis no trouble at all. Come, Miss Innes."

"But—"

He gave her a questioning look.

She stopped abruptly then heaved a great sigh. "Oh, never mind."

Gowan looked back, slack-jawed, as Morna followed with her escort. Gowan turned back to his guard. "Can't you see I was helping her? She'd have wandered off and got lost."

"'Tis not for me to decide. The laird will want to see you in the morning. You can explain it to him at that time."

The dungeon gate was at ground level, for which Gowan was grateful. It could have been some deep, dank oubliette. At least no rats were scurrying about—not that he'd seen or heard. Yet. He sat down and leaned his head back against the stone wall. If he'd struggled to sleep through the night in a comfortable bed, he had no chance of sleep in the dungeon, so he passed the time trying to understand how things had gone so terribly wrong.

His first mistake had been in assuming that Morna would be as agreeable as her brother. *Have I ever been so mistaken about anything?* Robert's request to "look out for my sister" should have been followed by "or she'll put a knife to your throat, ignore you through dinner, then have you thrown in the dungeon." Perhaps Robert was right to have left that part out. Dear friend's dying request or not,

Gowan would have thought twice—as he should have this evening.

Rather than chase after her, Gowan should have left her to fend for herself in the wild. With luck, she'd have gotten tangled in her skirts and fallen down close to the castle, to be found in the morning with her pretty ankles all swollen. At least with her immobilized, Gowan might have had a few days of peace. But he couldn't do that. He had grown up on the other side of those hills. While their beauty was staggering, they were harsh and unforgiving. As annoying as Morna could be, and no measurement existed to quantify that, she did not deserve a senseless death. He could not have stood by and let her put her life in peril.

Faced with the same choice, he would do it again. He would come to her aid again because that was the right thing to do. He had vowed to her brother he would keep her safe. But by God, that promise came with a price. For ruining her plans—whatever those were—she was making him pay. How long he would continue to pay would depend upon how cruel Robert's sister could be. And that remained to be seen.

GOWAN WAS SLUMPED over and dozing when the clink of a dungeon key woke him. He sprang to his feet and reflexively reached for his sword, but of course, it had been taken the previous night.

A guard stood at the open cell door. "The laird wishes to see you."

Gowan shielded his eyes from the bright morning sun

as he followed the guard to Malcolm's study. There, he found not only the laird but also Morna standing nearby, looking sheepish.

With a stern sideways glance at Morna, Malcolm said, "My daughter has something to say to you."

Gowan looked into her eyes. This was the other Morna, the meek, spiritless one he'd sat beside at supper. "Mr. Dunbar, I'm sorry. Last night, I didnae tell the truth about what happened, and I caused you to suffer a night in the dungeon unjustly. Please forgive me." With that said, her eyes settled on the carpet before her.

Eyeing her curiously, Gowan said, "Yes, of course."

Malcolm gave a nod to the guard who'd escorted Gowan there. He went at once to Morna and took hold of her arm. "Please come with me, Miss Innes."

As if she'd known this would happen, she put up no fight.

Seeing Gowan's questioning look, Malcolm explained. "She caused you to suffer a night in the dungeon. Now she'll do the same."

Gowan said, "Oh. But, my laird, that's not necessary." Lest his words come across too harshly, he smiled and added, "I've spent worse nights in the hold of a ship."

The guard hesitated in the doorway, watching the laird for further instructions, but the laird was unmoved. "She brought this upon herself." He nodded to the guard.

A pang of pity stirred in Gowan's chest. He couldn't help feeling sorry for Morna. While he could not deny his annoyance at having been tossed in the dungeon, he'd never feared for his life. Somehow, he'd believed it would all be sorted out in the morning. As frustrating as she could be, he did not believe Morna was cruel. Nor was

Malcolm—or so he had thought. The dungeon was no place for one's daughter, regardless of what she had done.

"You think me harsh?" Malcolm looked at Gowan curiously.

"I think she may have misunderstood my intentions last night. While I only sought to protect her, I can see how having a stranger in pursuit might have caused some concern."

Malcolm smiled, but it lasted only a moment. "You're a generous man, Mr. Dunbar. But this spirit of hers has caused problems before."

Gowan reminded himself that he'd only just met her. She clearly had a history. Yet surely Robert would have told Gowan if something about her was terrible enough to warrant a night in the dungeon, even if only for a night.

Malcolm went to the window. "As you know, 'tis a harsh world out there—too harsh for a girl to survive on reckless spirit alone. 'Tis my own fault. I should have provided her someone to teach her how to be a lady. She needed a mother, and I couldn't bring myself to provide her with one. While she did have a governess, the woman was far too lenient with her. She allowed her to play with her brother and encouraged the fanciful notion that she could lead the same sort of life as a man. Too late, I realized my error and dismissed the woman. But the damage was done. Now Morna thinks she can come and go as she pleases, deciding her fate with no care for how it might affect those around her. She's become rather mannish, sneaking out of the castle to wander about. 'Tis not right for a lass to behave so."

Gowan was feeling increasingly uncomfortable with what was clearly a very personal family matter. He reminded himself that, regardless of how he viewed the situation, it was not for him to agree or disagree with how a man ran his castle. Still, the poor lass deserved none of this.

Malcolm went to his desk and picked up Robert's letter. "It says here that Robert trusted you with his life. That is no small thing for him to have said. He gave you his trust, so now I shall do the same. I've an offer for you."

This was what Gowan had hoped for—a place to belong, to call home. Robert had been right. He'd felt almost certain his father would bring Gowan into the clan. With his military experience, he would be a welcome addition to the castle guard. It was the chance of a lifetime for the son of a crofter. He'd have a home and steady pay. Most of all, he'd be firmly planted within a community where he could belong and determine his future, something he'd never been able to do. It would be almost like having a family. Gowan's chest swelled with contentment as he waited to hear the laird's offer.

"I'd like you to be Morna's personal guard."

God help me. Morna's personal guard?

Malcolm said, "She told me that you were trying to protect her."

No good deed goes unpunished. It was all Gowan could do not to groan. He swallowed. "Thank you, sir. 'Tis an honor." *Not one I particularly wanted, but...* Gowan felt a frown forming and forced it away. He had promised Robert to look after her. *What better way?* While a smile was more than he could manage, he did his best to look dutifully pleased.

"You'll stay in Robert's room. It's the closest to Morna's. Your first job is to keep her safe—as you did last night. In addition, I want you to put a stop to this wild behavior of hers. She's not to go past the gates without escort or engage in anything else that's untoward."

So... no more day outings to undress completely and bathe in the river?

"Aye, sir. Shall I go now and release her from the dungeon?"

Malcolm looked at him with surprise. "Och, no. Leave her there for the night."

"For the night? Are you sure?" Gowan was hoping the laird might see reason upon second thought.

Instead, his eyes narrowed. "Did you not understand what I said? One thing you must learn and learn quickly —if I said it, I'm sure. You'd do well not to question me, lad."

"Aye, my laird."

Malcolm's face relaxed, and a light came into his eyes. "Good man." He gave Gowan's shoulder a pat and sent him out the door.

That was not at all what Gowan had expected. As he walked down the hallway, he silently vowed not to vow ever again.

Chapter Six

Clouds masked the sun, which had been so bright in the morning, as Gowan ambled down the path to the dungeon. He greeted the guard and asked if he might speak with Miss Innes. The guard tilted his head toward the corner of the cell, where Morna sat on a small stool.

She lifted her chin to look up at Gowan, her soft eyes shaded by a defeated expression. "Come to gloat, have you?"

Gowan stepped closer and touched his hand to one of the bars. It pained him to think she could believe him capable of it. "No. I came to tell you I'm sorry."

"Why should you be sorry? I did as much to you, did I not? If you managed a night here, I can as well." Her attempt at defiance was half-hearted.

Gowan said gently, "I never wanted this for you. What's more, I dinnae think you ever meant this for me."

She met his gaze with wide, honest eyes. "Perhaps you give me too much credit."

"Perhaps. Or perhaps I do not."

She again looked straight at him for a moment, then her eyes darted away. But in that fleeting moment, Gowan caught a rare glimpse of something soft and vulnerable. It moved him, but he was even more moved by her effort to conceal it. At the same time, he felt guilty for having seen it, knowing that it was not freely offered. Her present circumstances would tend to shed light on anyone's weakness, but she tried harder than most would to conceal it.

"Is there anything I can get you? Some food? You must be hungry."

"No, thank you." She folded her arms and would not meet his eyes.

Gowan gave a nod. "I ken that you're angry with me. If you'd rather, I can have someone from the kitchen deliver it."

Morna lifted her face but shut her eyes and leaned her head back on the stone wall behind her. She shook her head.

"At least have some water. I've got some here."

She slowly opened her eyes.

He counted it a great victory. "Here. I'd bring it to you, but..." He winced. The last thing she needed was a reminder of where she was. He took out his copper pocket canteen and held it toward her through the bars. He smiled as she uncorked it, but then she sniffed it, and he frowned.

"I said it was water." *Does she mistrust me that much?*

Satisfied that it was, she drank thirstily and returned the empty container to him.

"I can go get some more if you'd like."

She almost smiled as she shook her head—or maybe the sun was in her eyes.

Feeling suddenly awkward, Gowan lifted his eyebrows and exhaled. "Well, I'd best leave you to your... uh..." He went blank, distracted by the forlorn look on her face.

"Cold, stony cell to reflect upon my dismal life and my miserable fate?" She offered it with a hint of a smirk.

"Thoughts," he finished, now even more moved by the shimmering brown eyes that looked back at him. Had bars not been between them, he might have succumbed to an overwhelming urge to pull her into his arms... for comfort... on Robert's behalf. For despite their first meeting and the subsequent tension between them, he caught a glimpse of more tender emotions that tugged at his heart. He suddenly realized he was staring, and she was staring back. He broke the spell first. "I'm sorry."

Morna looked truly puzzled. "Why?"

Because I cannae help looking and longing... He shrugged and gave her the obvious answer. "Because you've been locked up unjustly, and you don't deserve this."

Her eyebrows drew together. "But you didn't deserve it, either."

"No."

She peered into his eyes. "I could've stopped it."

"Aye, well, I wouldnae have minded."

Light flickered in his eyes, but the next instant, it faded.

"I've brought something for you. I would have given it to you before now, but... I thought we might have a moment alone, but... I suppose this is it." He pulled a small folded piece of parchment from his sporran and handed it to her. "Before I gave Robert's sporran to your father, I took this from it. He doesnae strike me as a sentimental sort of man, so I didnae think he would miss it."

Morna gave her head a small shake as she unfolded the parchment, then she stared at its contents. Inside lay the remains of a pressed thistle. Her eyebrows drew together. She lifted tear-filled eyes to Gowan.

Gowan said, "I didnae ken whether it was yours, but I thought you might ken whose it was."

"It was mine. I gave this to him to remind him of home." She averted her eyes and wiped her tears away. "There's no value in it. Why would you bring it to me?"

"Because it had value to him."

"That's just blether." She shook her head and continued to avoid his gaze.

"Aye. I've a gift for it." He grinned, but she barely looked at him to see it. "Well, I'll leave you with that. Just remember that your time here will end soon enough."

"Oh, I doubt that. But end it will, and that's as good as it can be for the now."

He smiled and gave her a nod then walked away.

She called out, "Gowan?"

Hearing his name on her lips was surprise enough, but when he turned to see sincere gratitude, it disarmed him.

"Thank you."

He walked away wondering why, every time he laid eyes on her, it was as though he was meeting her for the first time—only not with a knife at his throat. And stranger still, each meeting only made him wish for more time to figure her out.

He would have that, thanks to the laird. He would have time to get to know her and time to understand how she'd managed to find a way into his thoughts. Not his heart. Thoughts were nowhere near the heart.

WITH THE FOG having lifted at last, Gowan mounted his horse and rode through the castle gate, urging his horse on through the wind to the top of the brae. He came to a halt at the top and looked down at the row of cottages he'd known since he was a child.

He knew which family lived in each cottage that lined both sides of the burn—except for one. The dwellings all followed the curve of the stream that cut through the glen. The croft that had once been his home had been rebuilt as though no flames had ever touched it. He could almost see his mother coming out of the door to call out for him. He still listened for the way she managed to make a song of his name. He'd been happy there once, oblivious to the troubles around him. But now his heart ached as his gaze followed the path he'd once walked to the kirkyard.

IT RAINED on the morning they buried Douglas Dunbar those five years past. Gowan still felt the weight of his father's coffin on his shoulder from when they carried him to the corner of the kirkyard preserved for his sort of sinner. Mist rose as if reaching up from the ground to pull him into its dark, peaty embrace. Unexpressed anger roiled within Gowan's heart as he walked home with the other men of their village. His mother was at home with the rest of the women. Her silence spoke more of her grief than anyone else could have managed with words. But they all felt it, the tragic injustice of dying like that.

Gowan's grandfather found him sitting on the stone wall at the end of the garden. He put a large, gnarled hand on Gowan's shoulder. The comforting strength of it made something catch in Gowan's chest. At seventeen, he was too old for weeping. When he'd tamped down his emotions, he turned to his grandfather. He'd never seen tears in his grandfather's eyes. He had to look away, lest his own overwhelm him.

When Gowan was able to speak, he said, "I dinnae ken why he had to die."

The old man frowned and nodded. "He was trying to protect your mother and you."

"Me? From what? I'm a man now. And surely the two of us could protect Mother."

"Aye." His grandfather gave Gowan's shoulder a pat. "But 'tis a sorrowful story to tell."

Gowan clenched his jaw as his sorrow gave way to anger. "Well, I ken how it ends. How much worse can it be?"

His grandfather cast a dark look his way. "From the time they were old enough to have such feelings, your father and mother were sweethearts. It was like they were born knowing that one day they'd marry. It's like that sometimes." He smiled, but it faded.

"The laird's son, Tasgall, took a fancy to Flora. I told your da to pay him no mind. After all, what else could he do? Our family had farmed this land for generations by the grace of the laird. The laird could take it away anytime if he chose, and we couldnae risk that. So your father did as I told him and looked the other way." Gowan's grandfather swallowed and did not speak for a while.

"Your father and mother were married. Och, the joy on their faces. You couldnae help but smile to see it. They were happy in those days, and Tasgall left them alone. He'd gotten over your mother, or so we all thought. Tasgall married. No one knows what went on between those two, but his poor bride looked miserable.

"One day at market, I caught him staring at your mother. I didnae say anything about it at first, but it happened again, and this time your father saw it, too. He started toward Tasgall. I gripped Douglas's arm and made some sort of excuse to send him in the other direction. It got so that when Tasgall was around, your father wouldnae leave your mother unless someone was with her. Time passed. Your father was careful and watched over your mother. Still, by that point, I suppose we all thought it was over.

"But one evening, Douglas was called to the castle. He was a bit late with his rent, so he went to discuss it. The laird was busy and unable to see him right away, so your father sat on a bench outside the great hall, and he waited. By the time the laird saw him, he asked Douglas what he'd come to see him about. The laird, it turned out, had never called him there. Your father left and ran back to the croft."

Gowan turned to his grandfather. "I remember the day. I was on my way back from fishing when I saw Da running home. I could tell something was wrong, so I ran too. When I got home, I found them both standing by the fire. Something was wrong, but they wouldnae tell me."

His grandfather gave a grim nod. "Tasgall had come to

the croft. He came in without warning. He was somehow convinced Flora wanted him too. Or maybe he didnae even care, the mad bastard. He forced himself on her, but she managed to push him away and run out of the croft to a neighbor."

Gowan said, "I remember Da loading a pistol. He said, 'Stay with your mother,' and left. There was a gunshot up near the castle. The next thing I knew, he was in the dungeon, and soon he would hang."

The old man sighed. "He would've murdered the laird's son, but the pistol misfired. I suppose the laird hoped your da would die in the dungeon so he wouldn't have to be responsible. Your father was well liked by all who met him, and the laird had to have known that his son was a monster. But it came down to them or us, and understand this... nobles will always close ranks and prevail. So when your father clung to life and wouldnae die quickly enough, they hanged him."

Gowan looked down at his former home and wondered how his parents' beauty and goodness had become their greatest misfortune. They'd wanted nothing more than to love one another, raise their family, and live out their lives in simple contentment. Even Tasgall had to have seen that. Perhaps that was what drew Tasgall in the first place. He saw the true love between them and thought he could take it for himself. But he could never have it, and that was his curse. For he couldn't understand that love like that could only be given, not taken. It was not his to possess. So instead, if Tasgall could not have her love, he'd have her.

On the next market day after his father had died, Gowan's mother sent him back on an errand for something she'd forgotten to buy at the market. He'd started to go when his mother called him back. She held onto his shoulders and looked into his eyes. "You've grown into a fine man like your father." She hugged him, which seemed a bit strange at the time. He was just going back to the market. But Gowan smiled and left, unaware that Tasgall had followed them home. His mother must have seen him following and lurking in the shadows of trees by the burn, for when Tasgall came into the house, she was ready with her husband's pistol in hand. This time, it did not misfire.

While Tasgall lay dying at her feet, she reloaded the pistol and left.

Gowan returned from his errand and found Tasgall dead. He and the neighbors all frantically searched for his mother. They found her at her husband's grave with a discharged pistol on the ground near her lifeless hand.

Gowan felt the loss keenly. His mother had been despondent over losing her husband. And she must have known it was only a matter of time before Tasgall returned. Gowan had seen the fear on her face every day, every time someone passed by too close to the cottage. His father had always been there to protect her. Gowan was there, but the loss of her husband must have left her inconsolable and facing a fear that would not end as long as Tasgall was near. In her weak moments, she had spoken of anger. Although she seldom spoke of her husband's death, Gowan had seen the cold look in her eyes whenever Tasgall's name was mentioned.

Some said she had planned it, while others were sure she could not have done it unless forced to defend herself against Tasgall's unwanted advances. Whether by design or in self-defense, she'd not only avenged her husband's death. She'd taken back control over her life and refused Tasgall the power he sought. Then she'd used it against him. And no one would hang her for her crime.

For her deed, Gowan's mother could not be buried on sacred ground, so they buried her outside of the kirkyard where the other sinners lay. A few days after that, when the full moon cast its light through gauzy gray clouds, Gowan rode down to the brae where his mother lay buried. He dug up her body and took her to the kirkyard. There, he dug up his father's grave and lay his mother beside him. The predawn light cast the world in a soft, silver haze as Gowan placed a small bundle of wildflowers on the grave of his parents. Then he mounted his horse, rode home and lingered long enough to set a torch to the croft, and rode away from the pain that was too much to bear.

For some time, he'd been thinking of going to war in search of adventure and fortune. He'd stayed for his mother, but since she was gone, there was nothing but pain for him there. So he set off, convinced he was not running away. This was no cowardly act. As a mercenary soldier, he would face the world bravely and make money to bring home and build a good life.

And he'd done just that. If his bravery turned out to be a mere mask for his anger and grief, no one would know the difference.

Chapter Seven

Gowan came back from the lists, where he'd spent most of the afternoon training. Malcolm Innes was a fair but demanding laird, and his guards reflected Malcolm's high level of discipline. As a result, Gowan had been put to the usual newcomer's test of proving his worth. But he knew his strengths and how to offset his weaknesses. In battle, his life had depended upon it. So he faced everything Malcolm's men put before him with the confidence of one who had been to war and had lost enough that nothing was left that could faze him.

He passed through the garden gate and stopped at the door to the kitchen. After spying the scullery maid, he casually leaned his shoulder against the doorframe. When she looked up from the table she was scrubbing, Gowan beckoned her over. She furrowed her eyebrows and glanced at the cook, who was giving directions to the kitchen maid.

Gowan leaned toward her. "I'm fair starving. Could

you wrap something up for me to take with me? I'm off for a ride." He looked into her eyes and smiled.

She smoothed strands of hair from her face and returned a shy smile. "I must ask the cook."

She scurried over to the cook, who looked in his direction. He grinned at her.

She looked directly at him then shrugged. "Och, dinnae waste your smiles on me, lad. You're a guest, so I'll get what you ask for, but if you make a habit of this, I'll be telling the laird you're the reason his supper's not ready." She instructed the kitchen maid to put together a bundle for him, then she barked at the gawking scullery maid to get back to work.

Gowan was barely past boyhood the first time he'd noticed the effect he had upon girls. His mother had noticed it too. With a stern look, she warned him that he would break hearts if he wasn't careful. "You've your father's braw build, and that light in those hazel eyes will charm all the lassies. Dinnae take advantage of it, or folk will think ill of you, Gowan."

He'd heard it from her more than once, so he felt a twinge of guilt as he smiled at the girl, and she blushed. But knowing the food was for a good cause, he took it and went on his way.

Darkness was falling, and he would soon be expected at supper. He went to the dungeon, handed a flask to the guard so he'd look the other way, then stood at the bars. "Miss Innes?"

She stopped pacing and turned.

"I've brought you some supper."

"Why?" She stared at him with an open expression that caught him off guard.

He had not been prepared for the question, instead anticipating a thank you, perhaps. "Why? Well, I suppose because I thought you might be..." His eyebrows drew together. "Are you not hungry?"

"Why would you care?"

"I recall what it's like in there. In fact, the memory's quite fresh."

She eyed him with mistrust.

He grinned and held the bundle through the bars. "We've all got to eat."

She eyed him again and looked at the bundle then took it and sat on the ground, where she opened it and began to eat. As she ate, she said, "I didnae bring you any food when you were locked in here."

"No. Maybe next time?"

Morna stopped eating and looked into his eyes then suddenly laughed. She returned to her eating while shaking her head.

Encouraged by her laughter, Gowan sat down by the dungeon door.

She looked up at him curiously then gestured toward the food. "Would you like some?"

"Och, no. 'Tis all yours."

She looked into his eyes and softly said, "Why?" Her eyes suddenly narrowed. "What's wrong with it?"

He laughed and caught her eye, prompting her to laugh too. She took a long drink.

Gowan said, "Do you think I would poison you?"

It took her a moment too long to reply. "No." Her mouth quirked at the corner. "'Tis too late now if you did."

His eyes were still lit from laughter as he gazed at her. His smile faded. "I give you my word, I'll not harm you."

She stared back in tacit acceptance, but doubt still clouded her eyes. "Why did you bring this to me? No one else cared to."

He shrugged. "I suppose I didnae think it was fair."

"I caused you to spend a night here, and now I'll spend a night in return. It sounds fair to me."

"Aye. But you didnae mean for it to happen."

"Are you trying to make me feel guilty?"

He drew his eyebrows together. "No. I was just doing a kindness."

She narrowed her eyes at him, but Gowan thought he detected a faint hint of mirth in them. He lifted an eyebrow. Those eyes of hers were quite something to look at. With the discipline of a warrior, Gowan tore his attention from her and refocused his thoughts on the matter at hand.

He opened his mouth to speak, but she heaved a sigh. "All I wanted was a few minutes alone."

Gowan frowned. "Outside? Alone? In the dark?"

"It's one of the few times I can be free. The truth is, I was saying goodbye to Robert."

"Forgive me if I repeat myself, but outside, alone, in the dark?"

"There's a place where we used to play when we were bairns. As we grew older, we'd go there to talk. The last time we talked, we sat in that spot. He'd lost Briana, and his heart was broken. He told me he was going away. So I gave him a thistle to remind him of home." She heaved a deep sigh. "All I wanted last night was to go there to say goodbye. Alone."

"Could I take you there—in the daylight?"

She cast a quick glance at him and shook her head. "Och, I ken that it wasnae your fault, but my grief isnae something that I want to share."

"I ken what it's like."

She gave him a questioning look.

"When I went to war, I'd just lost both my parents. I never had a moment alone till I left. In a way, that may have been good. But not at the time." He lost himself in dark reflection then remembered himself. "Your brother spoke of all this as something close to heaven."

Her lips spread into a gentle smile. "Aye, so it was— for him. But while he was outdoors with the other lads, busy with riding and archery, I was inside, being a lady." She rolled her eyes.

Gowan searched for the right thing to say. "I like ladies." That wasn't it.

She flashed a look of annoyance. "And knitting? Do you like that as well?" Before he could answer, she said, "Maybe you'd care to spend every day doing needlework and tending to the running of the house? How you men must envy us while you're out training then going off riding and hunting with the fresh Highland air in your chest and the mist on your face! Och, it must be so horrible for you—wishing you were back inside, bound by stone walls and stale air, immersed in the unfathomable joy of sticking one pointy thing into a loop then wrapping the yarn back around and slipping another over it and the needle." She put a hand to her chest. "Forgive me, my heart races just to think of the thrill."

Gowan's eyes twinkled as he smirked. "So you're not quite accomplished at it?"

She lifted her chin and stared with an unreadable expression. "The absolute worst you've ever seen. Holes, hanging bits and loops, and not one straight, even row to be found—it's just terrible!" She couldn't help but smile.

"Oh, lass, I'd be happy to help you sometime."

Her jaw dropped with shock. "You ken how to knit?"

He shrugged. "A bit. When you live in a croft, you learn to do a little of everything."

Frowning, Morna said, "I'm not sure I like you anymore."

His face brightened. "So that means you did? Like me... at one time?"

She smirked and turned away. "Dinnae let it go to your head. You've enough confidence, from what I can see."

"I'm sorry." And he sincerely was. All the women he'd known had been crofters, working outdoors and in. And while they had done their share of needlework, they also worked in the fields with the men and went out to the bogs to fetch peat to carry back. It was hard work, but perhaps it had its advantages, after all. He'd never thought about what life must be like as a young lady in a laird's house. Yet it was hard to muster too much sympathy for someone who came from so much wealth that her home and comfort were secured for the rest of her life.

But one question nagged at him. "My lady—"

"I'm not a proper lady. I'm just the laird's daughter."

"So... Miss Innes?"

"Morna. I think, at this point, dungeon etiquette rules apply."

"Aye, I suppose dungeons do tend to operate on a

given-name basis. But you do raise an interesting topic: the dungeon. Has this happened before?"

"Och, no. He just gave me the same punishment I inflicted on you. What bothers me more—other than not giving Robert a proper goodbye—is my complete lack of freedom." She turned to Gowan. "Apart from this, I still live in a dungeon. It's just a very large one."

"How so?"

"If I were a boy, no one would care if I went riding or hunting or fishing. But my father calls these my little acts of rebellion. And he's grown rather weary of them. When the guards found us together, my going out would have been just one more act of rebellion. I never meant to inconvenience you."

"Inconvenience? That's one way to describe it."

"Aye. I'm sorry. Truly I am. But they'd already seen us. There was no explanation that would have cast you in a favorable light."

"Except one."

In this dim light, he could not be sure, but he thought he detected a hint of guilt in her expression. "Aye. The truth would have been better. But all I could think of was how the guards would report to my father. So I thought if I shifted the blame to you, I'd escape one more reprimand."

"I see. But you didnae."

Her eyes widened. "No, I did. But I felt terrible about it. But I thought they'd just escort you to your room, then I could go on my way, as planned. But then one of them mentioned the dungeon, and it was too late. They took you, and... how could I stop them?"

Gowan lifted an eyebrow. "I dinnae ken. Maybe by telling the truth?"

"Aye. I should have. I couldnae live with what I'd done."

"Well, that's good. You deserved to feel guilty." Gowan took some pleasure in the fact that Morna looked duly miserable.

"I went to my father to tell him the truth right away, but he'd already gone to bed. So I went to bed—"

"I trust you slept well." He smiled wryly.

"I woke early—"

"Did you? So did I. Or was I already awake? It's all a nightmarish haze." He narrowed his eyes.

Morna winced. "I told him what happened as soon as I could. And well, here I am. And you've been so kind to bring me food. I ken that I dinnae deserve it."

Gowan folded his arms and regarded the woman. Everything that had happened between them should have made him dislike her. Yet he could not. At the same time, as much as he wanted to believe her, a thought came to him that he could not dispel. Perhaps she meant to manipulate him. Why wouldn't she seize the chance to take advantage of someone who clearly found her attractive? *For the love of God, King George, and whisky, lad, have you gone mad? You will not find her attractive. What would Robert think?* He cleared his throat as he gathered his senses. "Let us put this behind us."

She smiled, and it felt like the sun rising. "Does that mean you forgive me?" Since he'd met her, she hadn't smiled at him, not like this. But there she was. She'd let down her defenses to reveal a glimpse of the woman her brother had described.

Morna wiped her hands on the cloth that the food had come wrapped in and handed it back. But as she handed it to him, it fell. When she bent down to pick it up, she struck her head on the bars and let out a moan.

Gowan knelt down and lifted her chin to examine the injury. "Och, that's going to leave a mark." He brushed her hair back, but his touch made her wince. "Sorry, lass." Without thinking, he touched his hand to her cheek and gazed into her eyes. Something true passed between them in the silence that followed, and it was a frightening truth, evidently for both.

"You'd best go, or else..."

"Aye, or else..." Had bars not been between them, Gowan might have swept her into his arms and kissed her right there. She'd bewitched him. And he'd fallen for it. That wasn't like him.

Forcing himself back to his senses, Gowan stood up and held out his hand. She took it and stood then quickly withdrew her hand.

He nodded. "Aye, I'd best go before you put a dirk to my neck or have them put me in the dungeon, too." He grinned, but then he thought of how being inside the dungeon with her for a night might not be so bad, after all. *God pity me, she's done it again!*

"I'm sorry," she said softly.

Disarmed by her gentle sincerity, Gowan exhaled. "'Tis over, and all turned out well."

She frowned. "Aye. If you dinnae count the part about being locked in the dungeon."

His eyes lit, and he started to smile. "Och, well, there's that." He avoided her gaze until he could do so without smiling. But their eyes met, and they grinned at one another.

The guard cleared his throat loudly and, having gotten Gowan's attention, tipped the flask upside down. Gowan's bribe had run out. He turned to Morna and grinned. "I need a bigger flask."

"Now you'll ken better for the next time." She smiled.

"Next time?" He shook his head. "Let us not have a next time."

"'Tis not my first choice, mind you. But my choice has so little to do with how I pass my time."

He smiled. "I can think of far better ways to pass the time." His gaze swept over her hair and her face as he pondered the ways they could spend time together.

As if reading his mind, she looked down. He wasn't sure in this light, but he thought he detected new color in her cheeks.

Gowan came to his senses. "The time will pass, and you'll be out of here soon."

Her lips parted, and she took in a quick breath but stopped herself. "Thank you, Mr. Dunbar—Gowan." She looked down but then lifted her eyes again to meet his. "Truly."

The guard stood and headed toward him.

Gowan called to him, "Aye, I'm leaving." He glanced at her, grinned, and walked away.

Chapter Eight

Gowan returned to his room, unable to think of anything but Morna. He tried to understand how she could be so unhappy there. But then he thought of their supper together when they'd shared a meal and a good deal of silence. She'd spoken little more to her father. Although she'd been seated beside him, the laird barely acknowledged her presence. He had attributed it to her grief, but since he'd known her, no one had spoken more than a few words to her. She might as well have been invisible for all the attention anyone gave her. Perhaps she had brought that upon herself with her unapproachable manner. Or maybe her manner was the result of how she had been treated for years.

Still, Gowan wondered what, after she'd lived like this for her whole life, would drive her at that particular point to put herself in such danger. Yes, she'd wanted to say goodbye to Robert, but there must have been some way she might have managed it more safely. And aside from her nocturnal wandering, she'd roamed about unescorted before. Considering how he'd met her in the first place, he could not help but conclude that she must be in the habit of reckless behavior, gallivanting about the countryside as she did. Perhaps she hoped someone would notice. Even so, it was so lacking in judgment that she had to either be daft or wish herself dead. The thought struck him with sudden sadness. Moreover, it moved him to want to protect her from her own self-destruction.

But why should I? He had promised to look after her, not let her into his heart. In his defense, only a cold-hearted man would not be moved by a pretty young woman in peril. But duty came first, and his duty was to Robert and the vow he had made. Giving in to this relentless tug at his heart was entirely unnecessary. He was allowing his thoughts to stray. What mattered was that Robert's sister needed protection, and Gowan was there to provide it—no need to complicate matters.

AT LAST, morning came, and Morna's night in the dungeon was over. She longed to feel free, and the closest thing to it was riding. She longed to lean into the wind and feel the cool air toss her hair about with no care for whether she looked or behaved like a lady. Her heart quickened in anticipation as she strode to the stable.

Once there, in the stable doorway, she stood toe to toe with the head groom, a broad-shouldered man slightly taller than Morna with graying brown hair.

"What do you mean, I 'can't go riding'?"

"I'm sorry, miss, but the laird told me I'm not to allow you to ride anymore on your own."

Morna took a deep breath and exhaled. Anger had never served her well, so she forced herself to speak calmly. "Gerald, you taught me to ride. Surely you, of all people, know I can manage a horse on my own."

Gerald was not a demonstrative man, but Morna had known him for years, and she detected regret in his eyes. This restriction was none of his doing. Her father was punishing her, as if spending the night in the dungeon had not been enough.

"Is there a problem?"

Startled, Morna turned to find Gowan arriving at her side.

Gerald turned to Gowan. "No, there's no problem at all. May I help you?"

Flashing a warm smile, Gowan said, "I was thinking of going for a ride." He turned to Morna. "Perhaps you'd be so kind as to join me."

Morna's eyes widened, but she quickly concealed her reaction. "I'd be happy to." She turned to Gerald. "Surely my father would approve if I have an escort."

"Aye, miss, he would. I'll have your horses brought to you."

"Thank you, Gerald." As the head groom set about preparing Morna's horse, she said, "I'll finish here. You can get Mr. Dunbar's horse saddled."

"Och no, Sionn will be back soon."

The next moment, the stableboy returned from an errand and saddled Gowan's horse.

As Morna and Gowan rode out through the gate, she said, "You weren't going riding, were you?"

Gowan started to smile, but her stern look put that to a stop.

"Mr. Dunbar. I'll not suffer a liar."

"I heard your conversation, and I remember what you said about feeling trapped."

"Did I say trapped?"

"Something to that effect." He turned to focus straight ahead, and that was the end of the discussion.

Morna did not mind the silence as long as she controlled it, but as the morning wore on and Gowan's only words were of practical matters, she grew weary of it. She led the way into the woods, where they slowly progressed until the rush of water grew stronger. "There's a burn over here. We can water the horses."

When they arrived, Morna hurried to dismount before Gowan could reach her to offer help. She'd ridden there many times before unassisted, and it irked her that her father had instructed the head groom to refuse her the freedom to ride as she pleased. But in her haste to dismount, she neglected to notice her skirts getting caught in the saddle. She tugged, and it came free, but the sudden lack of resistance threw her off balance, and she fell backward. Braced to land on the gnarled tree roots below, she instead felt Gowan's arms around her. Startled, she looked up only to find him gazing back, inches from her.

"Are you all right?"

The ground could not have done a better job of knocking the wind out of her. His gaze wholly unsettled her, taking her breath and making her heart pound— which would not do. She made an ill-fated attempt to sound casual. "I'm fine. Put me down, please."

"Yes, of course." He set her down and held onto her shoulder while peering intently.

She could not trust herself to meet his eyes. Apparently, he had no such trouble. He bent his knees and looked up into her downcast eyes. The corner of his mouth was turned up as though he found her amusing.

"Thank you. If you'll excuse me." Morna took a few steps toward the water but still felt his presence acutely. She turned, fully expecting to find him staring at her. He was not. In fact, he'd disappeared. She looked about for him then waited until she could stand it no more. "Mr. Dunbar? Hello?" When no answer came, she called out again, this time louder. "Mr. Dunbar?"

"Aye? Is something wrong?"

She flinched and turned around to find him only a few feet away, adjusting his plaid. "Dinnae sneak up like that!"

"Sorry, but you sounded distressed."

She tried to act as though she had not been. She distractedly smoothed her hair back. "Not at all. I just... didnae ken where you were." She shrugged nonchalantly. "And I wanted to make sure you were all right."

He grinned and said, "Och, thank you."

She furrowed her eyebrows. "There's no need to thank me. I just wondered, was all."

It wasn't as though anything were wrong with the words. It was the way he said "thank you" that irked her. And that grin—it was as if he were trying to make her uneasy. He was good at it, so she'd have to do better at masking her feelings.

"Ah, well, since you were wondering, I had some personal business to attend to."

She shut her eyes. *Personal business. Of course.*

"If you'd care to..." He extended his arm.

"Yes, thank you. Excuse me." Morna walked away and

looked for a spot that might afford her some privacy. She and Robert had gone riding countless times and not had such an awkward time of it. This should be no different.

Gowan called out, "Dinnae go too far."

She answered from behind the trees, "I'll go as far as I like, so there's no need to further discuss it."

She returned to find him seated on a large boulder. With her hands on her hips, she said, "Ready?"

He looked at her. "There's no hurry. Come sit." He gave the rock a pat.

Unable to conjure an excuse not to, she reluctantly sat.

While Gowan watched the water trip over the rocks, Morna watched Gowan. He had a strong profile, with a nose that looked as though it had been broken at some point. The man had been to war, after all. If a broken nose was the worst thing he'd suffered, he could count himself lucky. Unlike her brother. Morna wondered why Gowan had been the one to survive and not Robert. She didn't like herself for having such thoughts, yet she couldn't seem to help it.

With his eyes still fixed on the water, Gowan said, "I should tell you that I didnae actually happen upon you by chance earlier at the stable."

Morna leaned away slightly. "Were you following me?" A shot of panic coursed through her. *Did he bring me out here alone, where no one can hear my cries for help?* She put her hand on the sgian-dubh she kept in her skirt pocket.

"I suppose I was."

She started for her horse, but he grasped her hand.

"Because your father asked me to."

She turned and looked at him, then her eyes trailed down to their clasped hands.

He followed her eyes and let go of her hand. "He's asked me to be your personal guard—to protect you."

Morna felt hurt and annoyed. "To protect me?" She rolled her eyes. "Aye. Because I need protecting. Why would he do that?"

Gowan winced. "Well, you've a wee history of running away."

"Running away? Is it so terrible to want just a small bit of time to myself where I can feel free? There's nothing so heavy as the weight of my father's expectations." She lifted her chin and clenched her hands at her sides. "Why you? He's got dozens of guards to choose from."

Gowan nodded in agreement. "I brought a letter to him from your brother. Robert's message seemed to have encouraged your father to have confidence in me. And... I was the only one who seemed to notice when you ran from the castle."

Morna rolled her eyes. "I see. So you happened to look out the window, and you were rewarded with the honor of nannying me."

Gowan shrugged as he fought off a smile. "Aye, something like that."

"And who's to protect you from me?"

He grinned. "I suppose I am at your mercy."

Ignoring how pleased he looked by the prospect, Morna said, "That doesnae explain why you accepted." She turned and leveled a frank look at him.

The amused light in his eyes faded. "Because I made a promise to Robert."

The look on his face made her forget the moment's frustration. She spoke softly. "A promise?"

"As he lay dying, he asked me to look after you, and I vowed that I would."

Morna took a few steps away, unable to tamp down a sudden surge of emotion. That sounded so like Robert. He had always looked after her. When her mother died giving birth to her, no other woman had been in the castle, at least not one with the power to make sure that Morna had a place in the family. She was the living reminder of something her father longed to forget, and she could see it every time he looked at her. So she'd been pushed to the outskirts of life in the castle.

Robert had saved her. He made her feel she belonged. Five years older than she was, he loved her and played with her. Any happiness in her childhood had come from him. Over the years, her brother had become very protective of her. He'd worried about leaving her home while he was gone, but she hadn't wanted to stand in his way. How she wished she had. She'd even envied him, wishing she could go with him to learn how to fight. Instead, he had learned how to die.

Morna took a breath and regained control, then she turned to face Gowan. "Robert trusted you?"

"Aye."

Their eyes met, and Morna felt somehow connected to Gowan. Robert had never been one to give trust or friendship lightly, so his trust in Gowan meant a great deal to Morna. "Well then, I suppose I must trust you, too."

As the two mounted their horses and headed for home, Morna felt a weight lift from her shoulders. Regardless of whether Gowan could improve her situation—and she doubted he could—simply knowing that Robert had tried meant the world to her.

ONCE HOME, they walked back from the stable and stopped outside Morna's room. Gowan was losing himself in her gentle gaze when a thought came to his mind, but he hesitated to voice it. "Miss Innes, I wonder if you're not too tired tomorrow..." He studied her to gauge her reaction. "I wonder if you'd like to go for a walk—in those hills you're so fond of."

She looked up at him, and a series of emotions passed over her face. He could only guess at surprise, confusion, and finally, curiosity. She seemed wholly unaware of how those gentle brown eyes shone when she answered. "Aye, I would like that."

Gowan was seized by an urge to lift her chin and put his lips upon hers. Instead, he forced a casual smile. "Good. Same time tomorrow, then?" He took in the light that shone from her eyes as she gave him a nod, then he walked down the hallway and tried not to smile too much.

Chapter Nine

The next morning, Gowan looked outside as rain drizzled down the glass pane of his bedroom window. He opened it and leaned out. A cold wind blew in from the sea, and the rain seemed to hang in the air before finding its way to the ground. This was the Scotland he remembered in its full brooding glory.

Personal guard or not, Morna's days of stealing away for a swim were over, for autumn's chill was upon them. Harvesttime had passed before Gowan arrived, and only the most tenacious rust-colored leaves clung to the trees. Gowan shut the window, sat down in the chair by the fire, and pulled on his boots. Morna would not like what he had to tell her. They would not go out walking today.

A knock sounded. Gowan opened the door to find the stableboy. "Sionn."

"The laird wishes to see you."

"When might the laird like to see me?" he asked, suspecting the answer.

"Now. He sent me to fetch you."

"Very well. I'll be along presently." Gowan started to close the door, but the boy took a step forward.

"I must bring you back with me."

"Aye?" Gowan stared down at the boy, who showed no sign of moving. "'Tis all right, lad. I ken the way."

"I must wait." He looked up at Gowan with unwavering confidence.

Gowan couldn't help but smile. "Aye? Well, wait there then."

He left the door open while he went back into his room and finished wrapping and pinning his plaid into place. After tying his hair back, he returned to the doorway and gave Sionn a nod then followed him down the hallway.

When Gowan walked into Malcolm's study, he found Morna there with the same blank expression she'd had during their first meal together. Their eyes met, and he sensed she was desperate to say something to him but couldn't.

Malcolm greeted Gowan then beckoned toward the window. Only then did Gowan notice a fourth person in the room, now walking over to join them. He was an imposing figure for a man of his age, which Gowan guessed to be well past his fiftieth year.

"William Huntly, allow me to introduce Gowan Dunbar."

The two shook hands amiably as Malcolm continued with the introduction. "Gowan was a trusted friend to my Robert, and that makes him practically family. He's been doing a fine job of looking after Morna."

"Not that I need looking after. I am a grown woman." The warmth of her smile did not reach as far as her eyes.

Malcolm chuckled, and Huntly joined in.

"She's a strong-willed lass, but we're working on that." Malcolm placed a firm hand on Huntly's shoulder. "Would you like a whisky, William?"

The two walked a few steps away and chatted while Malcolm poured four glasses of whisky. Morna took the opportunity to cast a wide-eyed look at Gowan, but he was at a loss as to how to interpret it.

Malcolm turned back, whiskies in hand, and offered Gowan a glass. When they all had whiskies, Malcolm cast a conspiratorial look at William Huntly. "We've been discussing the wedding and have decided there's no reason to delay. So the wedding will take place in a sennight."

Gowan's jaw practically dropped. He recalled talk of a wedding when he'd first met Morna, but it had not been mentioned since, so he'd assumed it would be some time before it took place. But he was even more shocked that Huntly was the groom. Of course, arranged marriages happened all the time among the titled and wealthy, and the ages did not always match. But Morna was too full of life to be wed to a man more than twice her age. It was so wrong for her. As if sensing his thoughts, Morna looked at Gowan, but she averted her eyes quickly.

Malcolm lifted his glass. "To the happy couple!"

Gowan went through the motions of toasting the couple, one half of which did not look very happy. Huntly went over to Morna, put his arm about her shoulders, and kissed her on the forehead.

Though Gowan caught himself wincing, he proceeded to force a congenial smile. As the shock subsided, he started to wonder why he'd been made privy to any of it, but his question was soon answered.

Malcolm turned from his conversation with Huntly and Morna and pulled Gowan aside. "I've offered your services to Huntly. You'll remain Morna's guard."

Having not been consulted, Gowan was taken aback. He felt like he'd been sold into servitude, but he heard Malcolm out.

"You're a fine guard, and you seem to get on with your duties better than anyone else has. You've gathered by now that our Morna's a spirited lass, and I worry about her. We can't very well have her wandering off when she's married. While he doesnae ken my specific concerns, Huntly is amenable to the arrangement. I can't imagine it would make any difference to you here or there. So if you are agreeable, after the wedding, you'll go along to Huntly Castle as Morna's personal guard."

Gowan was still digesting it all when Malcolm clapped a hand on his shoulder. "Give it some thought. 'Tis a good position for you, and as you have no home, you're the most likely man here for the job."

When Gowan managed a stunned nod, Malcolm returned to the others. Gowan threw back his whisky and went to the window to stare at the rain falling down on the land that he'd hoped would be his new home.

Morna walked over to him and said softly, "I'm leaving. You're welcome to follow."

He turned to find Morna making her way across the room to her father and Huntly. She spoke softly as she put her fingertips to her forehead with a pained expression and headed out of the room. Gowan offered a quick bow to the others and followed her out like a dutiful guard.

Chapter Ten

Morna went to her room knowing Gowan would follow. She opened the door and waited for him. When he arrived, she hooked her arm about his and dragged him inside.

"What the devil? I thought you were ill."

"I had to get out of there."

He shook his head. "I cannae be in your chamber like this."

Morna looked frantically at him. "He kissed me."

"Huntly?"

"Who else?"

"No one. I just wasn't expecting it of him. How? Your father was there."

"He kissed me hello."

"Och, I dinnae think you can count that as a kiss. Not a real one."

"It was awful, and I cannae bear it again."

"If you're going to marry the man, there might be kissing."

Morna shook her head. "I'll marry him, but I'll have no more of that."

Gowan winced. "Sooner or later, he'll want to. And... you ken that there's more to it..."

"Aye." Her face could not have wrinkled up more. "Let's run away!"

"What?"

"We could steal away this evening. I know a secret way out of the castle—a tunnel. I'll say I'm too sick for supper, and you'll stay behind to guard me, then as soon as they've gone down, we'll leave. Oh, but we'll need some horses. Never mind, I'll figure out something. We can pretend we're going out for a ride. Oh, but it'll be after dark. I know, I'll make up some sort of excuse—an emergency trip to fetch the doctor."

"No." His eyes fixed on hers.

"Did you see him?" She looked up at him, desperate to be understood.

"Mr. Huntly? I did."

"Well, then you know I cannae marry him!"

"Do I?" The confused frown on his face offered no encouragement.

Morna took a deep breath and exhaled, trying to hang on to her last bit of patience. "He's older than my father. And he's got hair growing out of his nose."

Gowan started to smile. "Oh, aye, that's a dreadful affliction."

"We cannot be married. Surely you can see that."

"But you've already agreed."

She rolled her eyes then looked pointedly at him. "In this family, we dinnae agree. We obey." Morna started to pace. "I thought I could do it. And it seemed like such a long way off—months. But now he wants to move it up to a sennight from now! I dinnae think I can do it. I *know* I cannae do it."

Gowan stared sympathetically but said nothing.

"Well?"

"Well what? Lass, I'm sorry, but there's naught I can do. You've made a promise to marry him."

Morna stopped pacing and stood facing him. "*My father* made the promise."

"Either way, the promise has been made, and it cannae be undone." He put comforting hands on her shoulders and peered into her eyes. "It might not be so bad. And you heard your father. I'll be with you."

"Except in my bed—" She stopped, but it was too late, so she looked straight at him. "That's not what I meant. I meant you willnae be able to stop it. He'll want to... touch me..." She turned away and shuddered. "I cannae do it."

"Miss Innes."

Something about his formality, coming right after such a personal confession, irked her. "Could you not call me Morna, at least?" Frustrated, she turned and looked into his eyes. His gaze softened. The sympathy she found there melted her defenses, and tears came into her eyes.

"Morna." He wrapped his arms about her and held her, just for a moment, then lifted her chin. Their lips parted, then he kissed her on the forehead and released her, stepping back to arm's length. "I'm sorry. I shouldnae have done that."

She looked at him as though she'd never seen him. Still stunned from his kiss, she said, "I didnae mind it." But she could see the regret on his face. The way he averted his eyes made it clear he felt as awkward as she did. But she had to press on. They might not have another chance to talk alone. "I just thought, for Robert's sake, you might take me away."

The power of invoking her brother's name registered on his face, but he shook his head slowly. "Think about what you're asking and what you'd be doing. You've just lost your brother. Are you really prepared to lose your father, as well? You must ken if you leave here you couldnae come back."

The point struck a harsh blow.

Gowan went on. "You'd be alone. And whatever you managed to take with you to live on would only last so long. Highway robbers could steal it. Or worse. Then where would you be? How would you live?

"Is that any worse than being trapped in a stranger's house, forced to do as he wishes?"

"Aye, I believe it could be."

Morna shook her head vehemently. "I cannae see how. But I can see it was foolish for me to ask you for help."

"Not foolish at all, just an ill-advised plan."

All hope was lost. Morna slowly nodded. "I see. Well, I thank you for listening to my mad ravings."

Aside from looking thoroughly uncomfortable, he managed to look kind. "They're not mad ravings. They're just not what's best for you."

"Everyone seems to ken what's best for me, yet no one considers my feelings."

He took her hand in both of his. "Miss Innes— Morna, I cannae change what's been decided, but I will do everything that I can to make it easier for you."

His hands felt so warm and strong about hers, but it wasn't enough. He was not going to help her. She was on her own now. "Thank you... for listening." She lifted her eyes.

He smiled gently and gave her hand a comforting squeeze then went to the door. Just as he reached for the door, a knock sounded. He pulled his hand back as if he'd just touched hot embers. Their eyes locked with panic, then she frantically beckoned him to the bed. He looked at the bed, then at her, with alarm.

A knock sounded again, and her father called out. "Morna, are you in there?

Morna frantically whispered, "You cannae be in here."

"I believe I said that."

Her father called out again. "Morna, are you in there?"

She frantically whispered, "Hide under the bed."

The knock turned to pounding. "Morna, are you all right?"

"Yes, Father, I'm coming." She opened the door, smoothing her hair. "Sorry. I was resting."

"Ah, yes. How's your head?" Without waiting for an answer, he said, "Where's Dunbar? He's supposed to be guarding you."

"He is."

"Where?"

"Yes, well, earlier... 'Tis my own fault. I was taking my hair down while I looked out the window, and I dropped my comb outside. Mr. Dunbar is retrieving it for me."

"I see. Mr. Huntly was hoping to spend some time with you. He's just back from Aberdeen and rode straight here to see you."

"I'm so sorry. Perhaps I'll be better in time for supper."

"See that you are. Dinnae make fools of us, Morna."

She nodded and walked her father to the door.

Turning, he gave her a kiss on the forehead. "I'll see you at supper."

"Aye, Father."

She closed the door and rushed to the bed. "You can come out now." Gowan pulled himself out from under the bed and stood, brushing the dust from his plaid.

"Och, I'm so sorry!" Morna started to brush off the dust from his plaid, but Gowan gripped her hand and pulled it out of reach.

"Stop. I can manage." He finished dusting himself, gave her a nod, then left for his post safely on the other side of her door.

GOWAN CLOSED the door and exhaled. That was a low point, not only because he had hidden under a woman's bed while her father walked about her bedroom but also because he had unwittingly found himself in a compromising position, at a loss for a remedy. Mistakes like that cost men their lives.

Still, the lass deserved better than the lot she had drawn. And if he were in a position to help her, he would. But he wasn't. Short of sweeping her onto a horse and riding off with her, and risking his life in the process, he could do nothing. While he felt for her, having to marry a man twice or thrice her age, Gowan could not compromise himself again.

Yet he could not help but wonder what it would be like to run away with her, riding alongside her while the wild Scottish wind blew through her long silken tresses. Perhaps they'd stop at an unoccupied bothy to rest. He'd build a fire, and she'd stand before its amber glow and let her hair down to dry. He'd join her there to circle his arms about her waist, and he'd bury his face in her neck and press his lips to the smooth slope of skin that led down to her shoulder, then spin her around and put his lips on hers. And she'd kiss him and tell him how much better this life was than the life they'd left behind. And she'd be right. A man could fall in love with a woman like that.

Gowan shook his head in disgust with himself. The truth was he'd been denying his interest in her. *Interest?* He wanted her so much that he ached. He'd tried to convince himself that he was there to take the place of her brother as much as he could. That was how it was meant to be, so he convinced himself that was how it was. Any feelings he had were merely brotherly concern—the kind in which he'd gazed into her eyes, and his eyes would sweep down her soft cheek to her lips, and he'd wonder what her body would feel like against his.

He leaned back against the stone wall and shook his head. Robert had not sent him here to lust after his sister. *Why* did *he send me here?* Perhaps it was simply to look after his sister, but Gowan wondered whether Robert had known about the arrangement with Huntly. If he had known, it made sense to send Gowan to do something about it. What that was, Gowan did not know. He had no power to stop it. He couldn't have expected Gowan to abscond with his sister. Men had been hanged for less. *Did Robert intend to risk my life?* Gowan was not one to speak ill of the dead, but if that were the case, he had a few thoughts for Robert that were best left unsaid... or unthought.

GOWAN WAS SEATED for supper at the end of the dais when Morna arrived. He'd been displaced from his usual seat to make room for Huntly. Which was as it should be, Gowan reminded himself. He was fine down there at the end of a very long table. He had a tankard of ale, and a good meal would soon be before him. At least it looked like a good meal from this distance.

Then Morna walked in, and Gowan forgot how to breathe for a moment. He saw no sign of the strain that had shown on her face when he'd left her. In fact, she was practically glowing. Her hair was brushed into smooth, shining strands all drawn back in plaits to reveal the satiny slope of her neck to her shoulders.

Huntly stood and said something quietly to her. Morna managed a smile as she nodded. The man was not a beast. He seemed kind enough to her. Morna could do worse. And after all, marriage was not about love at her social level. It was a contract meant to form alliances that would strengthen their stance in the region. Love was a privilege reserved for the poor—except in the case of his parents. People like them, like Gowan, were subject to the whims of the landowners. His parents' mistake was in thinking that love conquered all. Love conquered nothing but one's better judgment, and in his parents' case, such judgment had cost them their lives.

Not long after losing his parents, he'd found a good friend in Robert Innes, a man who'd left home because he was in love with a woman he could not have... another mistaken decision for which Robert had paid with his life. Gowan, instead, would live his life alone rather than go through any more loss or unhappiness. He would take pleasure where offered and leave love for those whose bold hearts outweighed their good sense.

And Morna... what she wanted was really no different from what Gowan sought—control over one's heart and one's life. She had not asked for love, only escape. He couldn't really fault her for that. From his place at the end of the dais, he could only catch glimpses of her as she politely conversed with her husband-to-be. But her lovely soft gaze was wasted on Huntly. She held back the warmth and the fire that Gowan so enjoyed. William Huntly would never see the sparks fly when her unbridled spirit came up against his. Gowan felt a bit selfish about that, for as frustrating as he found her at such times, the sparks landed on him, and he willingly burned just for her. *Does she feel it too? Does she know that's what's missing with Huntly?*

Gowan shuddered to think of Morna with Huntly... together. He composed himself. Those two were going to be married. Perhaps in time, they might find common ground, some contentment. He hoped so for her sake. She deserved to be happy.

Which was why, no matter how persuasive Morna's soft gaze could be, he would not succumb to her pleas of escape. Everyone had to face unpleasant tasks at some point in their life. Gowan never enjoyed running into battle, but he had made the commitment, so he had done it. Morna would develop her own skills for survival. And they'd both be better off for it.

Chapter Eleven

Gowan suffered through a breakfast in which he unavoidably endured the sight of Huntly trying too hard to charm Morna... and failing. Despite Huntly's physically imposing presence, his efforts to woo Morna left him looking helpless and weak. Shakespeare was right—love made fools of us all.

For Morna's part, while she did not appear overly warm, she at least appeared pleasant. If it was grounded in obligation or pity, Huntly seemed unaware. Only Gowan, who knew that she barely tolerated the man. Only he could imagine her struggle.

After breakfast, Huntly took Morna's hand. "Mr. Dunbar, would you see to our horses? Miss Innes and I are going out for a ride."

Gowan took a moment. "As Miss Innes's personal guard, I cannae desert my post to run errands."

"I'll go with you!" Morna said cheerily, if a little too quickly.

Gowan smiled at Huntly. "Ah, there we are. Both purposes served."

Huntly did not look pleased, but before he could offer a better alternative, Gowan turned to Morna and gestured for her to proceed.

As they stepped outside, Morna heaved a great sigh. "Och! A breath of fresh air and freedom!"

Gowan turned toward her, concerned that someone might have heard.

But before he could say anything, Morna laughed and took off in a run toward the stables. "Come on! I'll race you!"

He ran after her and caught up as they reached the stable.

Morna stopped at the first stall and turned, beaming as she caught her breath. "I won!"

Gowan joined her and leaned against the stall door. "I beg to differ. You had a head start, and I actually caught up to you at the end." He assumed an indignant expression, but a smile won out as he caught her eye.

She leaned close and said softly, "If we hurried, we could saddle the horses and be gone before he got out here!"

Although tempted, Gowan said, "But that would be cruel."

Morna sighed. "Aye, you're right. But he is such an odious man, and I cannae abide with the touching." She wrinkled her nose. "This morning, he caught me off guard, and he kissed me."

The news angered Gowan more than it should have. "When? I've been watching you two like a hawk." *Which has gone beyond duty and passed into the realm of the pathetic.*

"Have you?" Morna looked surprised, almost pleasantly so.

"Aye, well, it's my job, after all. You haven't answered my question."

"We were on our way in to breakfast when one of the other guards stopped you to talk about something."

Gowan recalled it. It had taken no more than a minute.

"When he pulled you aside, Huntly pulled me into a window alcove and pressed his mouth to mine before I could pull away. I thank God you caught up with us."

"I had no idea." Had Gowan seen it, he might have been tempted to plant his fist in Huntly's face. Which would have been a slight overreaction under the circumstances. "It's not like him to be so impulsive."

"Aye. He said something about being overwhelmed with happiness... couldn't control himself... couldn't wait for the wedding." She set sad, round, brown eyes on Gowan and practically pouted.

It was all he could do to refrain from voicing his thoughts lest his anger, and other emotions, become too apparent. A man wanting to kiss the woman he was going to marry in less than a sennight was to be expected. However, for the young lady's personal guard to feel rage at the prospect was out of the ordinary. But upcoming nuptials or not, the bride deserved some sort of say in the matter.

Morna said softly, "I always thought that a kiss would feel... different."

Gowan's face went blank. He leaned closer and said softly, "Was Huntly the first?"

She managed a reluctant nod.

He gazed down at her lips as he quietly said, "Aye, a kiss should... feel different."

Morna lifted her eyes, and they became locked in a gaze that neither seemed able to escape. A pang of regret was cast aside by fervent need. Pulled by forces neither could resist, they drew closer together, lips parting.

"Halloo!" Huntly called out as he neared the stable.

Gowan pulled Morna into the shadowy corner and turned as he reached out an arm to pull her behind him. Huntly ducked his head inside the stable and called again as he glanced about, squinting.

"Over here!" the head groom yelled from the other direction as he rounded the opposite corner.

Huntly went to meet him, no doubt to ask why the horses were not already saddled, for the head groom called out, and two stableboys ran inside and began saddling horses.

Gowan set about saddling his own while Morna slipped outside unseen and took the long way around the stable.

A MINUTE LATER, she rounded the far corner and walked over to Huntly and the head groom. "Ah, there you are."

Huntly nodded, but his face was clouded with suspicion. "Where have you been?"

She lifted her eyebrows. "Well... I was... I stopped to admire the weather this morning."

He accepted her explanation in part. "But where is your guard?"

Morna panicked. She opened her mouth, hoping an answer might come to mind. It did not. "Oh, well... he's..."

"Saddling my horse." Out came Gowan with his horse, followed by two stableboys with the others.

Huntly turned to look while Morna exhaled with relief.

Huntly's eyes narrowed. "For someone who refused to let this lady out of your sight, you seem to have abandoned her to wander about by herself."

Morna walked over to Huntly. "Oh, no, he didnae abandon me. I insisted."

Unconvinced, Huntly frowned.

She nodded. "I had... uh..." She leaned closer and whispered, "Lady business."

He turned with a frown. "What?" His face reddened. "Oh. Uh... well... uh..." He looked about, clearly flustered. "How are those other two horses coming along?"

"Right here, sir," said a stableboy standing before him, reins in hand.

Huntly cleared his throat and turned, ready to help Morna into the saddle, but Gowan got to her first. He and Gowan mounted their horses, and Huntly took the lead.

"Let's go then, shall we?"

Morna and Gowan exchanged relieved glances, and the three rode away.

THEY'D BEEN RIDING for over an hour when Morna spoke her first words of substance since setting out from home. "There's a burn over there. 'Tis a good place to rest and water the horses."

"Och, they're fine." Huntly patted his horse on the neck.

"But I need a rest." Her eyes flitted back toward Gowan, who was riding discreetly behind. It was such a small glance, but it was the first contact of any sort he'd had with her since their moment in the stable. He wasn't quite sure what she thought, whether she was angry with him or riddled with remorse. Worse yet, perhaps he had misread her and made the same error as Huntly. That thought pained him the most.

Gowan followed the couple as they dismounted and walked their horses to the stream. As soon as he was able, Gowan excused himself and disappeared into the woods to relieve himself. When he'd finished, he turned toward the rustle of footsteps on fallen leaves. "Morna—Miss Innes." He made a face when he realized he'd called her by her first name, which he never did in the presence of others. He called a bit more loudly, "Miss Innes, is that you? Mr. Huntly?"

He heard a grunt of distress and took off running toward the sound. "Miss Innes!"

"Dinnae fash! She's with me."

"I'd rather hear that from her." Gowan followed Huntly's voice until he found them together in a tight embrace.

Huntly smiled. "As you can see, she is fine."

"I am *not*." Her eyes burned with no less rage than he'd seen on the battlefield.

Huntly grinned. "God in Heaven, lass, can't a man kiss his bride?" He looked at Morna then tossed a conspiratorial grin in Gowan's direction. "Timid lass. I'll cure that."

Gowan gave him a courteous smile then turned to Morna. "Miss Innes, would you mind seeing how the horses fare?"

That raised Huntly's ire. "She'll not take orders from you."

"No, but I'd like a word with you, sir." He fixed his eyes on Morna. "Miss Innes?"

With a nod, she extricated herself from Huntly's embrace and went down to the stream.

Gowan spoke in measured tones. "Sir, you ken that part of my job is to keep the Mistress Innes's virtue intact. The lady isnae your bride yet. I fear the laird would not look kindly upon these impassioned overtures."

"One overture. I embraced my future bride."

"And tried to kiss her before breakfast."

Huntly's nostrils flared. "You're spying on us?"

Gowan leveled a look. "It's my job." He ignored Huntly's glare and went to help Morna with the horses.

She would not look at him. "You left me alone."

With only a few seconds before Huntly would catch up, Gowan paused before helping her mount her horse. "And you're angry with me."

Glaring at him, she said, "Aren't you observant."

"I'm sorry."

Morna glanced toward the approaching Huntly then took hold of the reins and led their two horses away from the stream.

Gowan burned with conflicting emotions. He was

angry with himself, with Huntly, and with the situation. He helped Morna onto her horse, wrapped a hand gently around her ankle, and looked up at her. "I'll not leave you again."

As she looked down at him, her anger melted into despair. "Until the wedding night."

Huntly joined them, and Gowan left Morna's side to swing up onto his horse. He followed the pair as they rode side by side, and he still felt the sting of pain in Morna's gaze. The woman he'd met, once full of strength and spirit, was fading before him.

Gowan smiled as he recalled meeting her—and her knife. She was quite handy with that. A wild ride across Scotland with her would have been quite an adventure. His smile faded as he thought of the life waiting for her instead. He shook his head. He had no right to feel this way, but it was too late. *When had this happened?*

For the rest of the day, Gowan was true to his word. He never left her alone. But he did so at a distance. Morna Innes had her own life to live, and he had no part in it.

THEY MADE it through supper and its uncomfortable silence peppered with an occasional awkward exchange. After that, they all retired to the parlor, where Gowan settled into a window seat, book in hand, apparently doing his best to remain as far from any of them as he could.

Morna could hardly blame him. She'd practically thrown herself at him in the stable. *But is it so wrong to long to be kissed—really kissed—by someone... someone who...?* She put the book she'd been trying to read in front of her face, fearing someone might be able to tell just by looking at her that she'd fallen in love. *Oh, Morna. You're too smart for this. Yet how smart could I be to have let myself get into this situation?* She should have pressed harder against the idea when her father had first brought it up. She could not—would not—marry Huntly. It just could not be.

Huntly turned from the fire, where he and Malcolm had been talking. "Morna?"

She lowered the book and looked up abstractedly.

"Do you play chess?"

She shook her head demurely and lied, "No, not really... very well."

Her father cast a sharp glare her way, for he'd taught her to play.

Her eyes brightened. "My father plays, though."

Malcolm let her get away with her lie, no doubt for the sake of his guest, and joined Huntly at the table and arranged the chessmen on the board.

Huntly didn't seem very happy about the change in partners, but Morna had left him no option but to play the game with her father or appear rude. While they played, she took a turn around the room and paused close to Gowan to gaze out the window into the dark night. She thought her mere presence would at least draw a glance, but his eyes remained fixed on his book. She let out a soft sigh.

Huntly called to her, "Morna, come here. I'll show you how to play—for those long winter evenings together."

She clenched her jaw and went over to the table,

where Huntly went down the list of kings, queens, bish-
ops, knights, rooks, and pawns. She made the mistake of
looking at her father, who lifted an eyebrow and
suppressed a grin that more or less told her she deserved
what she was getting, a lecture in the rudiments of a game
she knew well.

When Huntly had finished, Morna said, "Thank you!
But I've fallen behind in my knitting. If you'll excuse me."

She got up and retrieved the same project she'd been
working on for the past several months. Whenever Huntly
turned toward her, she drew her eyebrows together and
made a good show of clicking the tips of the needles
together.

Chapter Twelve

A wooden door scraped closed. Gowan sat up in bed and turned his ear toward the sound of light footsteps as they padded down the hallway. He leapt out of bed, tossed the loose end of his plaid over his shoulder, and quietly opened his door. When he was sure no one was waiting to clobber him over the head, he ran straight to Morna's room. She was gone, and he felt the same sinking gut feeling that used to plague him before battle.

He ran down the hall in the direction of the footsteps. When he reached the stairs, he had to choose whether to go down the winding stone stairway or to go a few steps up to the door that led to the battlement. He stood still and listened. A muffled sound, a missed step, and a grunt came from above, so he went to the door, pulled on the handle, quietly slipped outside, and closed the door behind him.

The sliver of moon was no help in the pitch-black night, so he felt his way along the walkway before him. Alert to any movement, he stepped quietly. He hoped the light wind had masked the sound of the door, but he had to expect that whoever was out there had the advantage of knowing of Gowan's presence, if not his precise location at this moment.

A flag flapped in the wind. Gowan turned toward the noise and saw something halfway down the battlement. In the shadows, he spied a lone figure that stood looking out through the crenel with arms stretched out to the side. The wind masked the sound of his footsteps as he drew closer. The figure was too slender to be one of the guards. *Morna, no.*

She did not hear him until he was inches from her, but by then it was too late. Gowan hooked his arm about her waist and pivoted away until his back hit the merlon. Once she was safely away from the opening, he held her to make sure she stayed that way. But as he held her, he found that he couldn't let go—not only for safety, but also because he didn't want to.

She'd stolen away to come up there. Gowan didn't need to ask why. He just held her against him so closely that he felt her heart pound against his chest. Cradling her head in his hand, he spoke softly. "Lass, what were you doing?"

Her tears moistened his cheek. "I wasnae going to jump. Not tonight. I just wanted to see if I could... if I had to."

He looked up at the sky. "You can't. I won't let you."

She buried her face in his chest. "I don't want to. I want to live. And I want to love."

Gowan wanted to say that she would. He wanted to promise her a full life and great love. But he couldn't.

Morna wiped her face. "This isn't like me. I've always

thought I'd have control of my life, that I wouldn't have to be like other women I see. But then I sat in the parlor, cowering with my knitting—I hate knitting—just to give me an excuse to avoid him. My husband-to-be. And I realized then that this was my life-to-be. And I couldn't bear it."

"Och, lass." Gowan held her against him and smoothed her hair, breathing in her scent.

"I just needed to know that I had a way out. I don't want it. I just need to know that it's there."

He took her face in his hands. "That is not your way out."

When he heard the guard walking down the parapet, Gowan turned, took her hand, and led her to the door, where they ducked inside. "Let's go someplace where we can talk."

Morna nodded, and they went down the stairs then stopped. She lifted her eyes with a questioning look.

Gowan thought about where they might talk without being disturbed. His room was the closest, and hers was the next one down the hall. Neither would do. Yet those would be the easiest to slip in and out of.

She whispered, "Your room. It's closer."

Even as he agreed, he knew he was taking a foolhardy risk, but he ignored his gut feeling. They made it safely down the hall to his room. As soon as the latch slipped into place, Gowan headed for the window with the sole thought of putting distance between them. Morna sat in the chair by the fireplace and stared at the embers.

What seemed like a long time passed while Gowan stared out the window into the dark night and wondered what he thought he could say or do to solve her dilemma.

But it was not just a dilemma—it was her life. Still unsure of the best thing to do, Gowan turned toward her and leaned on the window ledge. "You've got your whole life ahead of you."

"I've got *a* life. But it isnae *my* life—not the one I'd have chosen."

Gowan ventured closer and leaned on the mantel. "What do you want? What's the life that you thought you would have?"

She smiled softly and leaned her head back against the chair. "I had it. Before Robert left, we used to go riding and have our own archery contests. In the summers, we'd go swimming and hike in the hills. In the winters, we read and played chess. He was clever and fun. We'd laugh, and we'd argue. And when he fell in love, we'd ride off together, then I'd go off on my own while he snuck off to meet Briana. All the while, I was sure that the same thing would happen to me. I'd fall in love and be as happy as he was. Life seemed so simple and good back then. I was free to do what I wanted. No one cared what I did or where I went. My father just left me alone... until Robert left, and my father decided that I should be married. And everything changed."

Gowan smiled and pulled a small stool over and sat down next to Morna. "I felt the same way after I lost my parents."

"I'm sorry."

"Aye. My parents and my home. At the time, I thought my life had ended. That was why I went off to war. It was hard, yet it was simple. I just had to think about eating and sleeping and fighting. I met your brother, and we became friends. To look at us, you would think we had nothing in common, but we had everything in common that mattered. We'd both lost people who were dear to us, and we were both running away. We became like brothers. Even now that he's gone, he continues to make my life better."

Morna leaned closer to Gowan and smiled. "That is so like Robert. Always thinking of others. He helped me to think big and to dream. I miss him."

Gowan put his hand on hers and gave it a squeeze. "I cannae replace Robert, but I'm here."

She gazed into his eyes. "You are, and I'm glad that you are. But once I'm Huntly's wife, it won't be the same." She sighed. "Everything changes."

"I cannae stop the wedding. It's not my place. But I'll be there as your guard. If he ever tries to hurt you, I promise I'll protect you."

"Thank you. I dinnae think he would hurt me. Maybe bore me to death." She tried to smile, but tears moistened her eyes. "I just wish..." She stood up. "I should go back to my room."

She turned to leave, but Gowan stood and grasped her hand. "What do you wish?" He grinned playfully. "I promise I won't tell anyone."

Morna gazed into his eyes for a moment, then she looked away. "I wish... Robert died having known love. I'll never have that. Or the thrill of a kiss." She looked down at their clasped hands and slowly slipped hers from his. "More dreams to let go of." Shrugging, she turned away to stare at the dying coals in the fireplace.

"It's a kiss that you dream of?"

She whispered, "Your kiss." Morna couldn't turn around to see his reaction. Perhaps it was easier that way.

She had said it. His silence was answer enough. She had to leave.

He touched her shoulder and turned her around. She couldn't bring herself to look at him, but he touched her chin and lifted it so she couldn't help but see him bend down to her. His lips touched hers, lightly at first, then he pulled her against him and kissed her fully. It was more of a thrill than she'd even dreamed it might be. Her heart could break from the joy of his warmth and his strong arms about her.

Between kisses, she whispered, "I just want to remember—"

"I know." He kissed her again and stroked her hair then clutched her against him.

MORNA'S HEAD swam from the surge of conflicting emotions. Their kiss was more than she'd dreamed it could be. She told herself it would only happen once. After that and as long as she lived, she would always remember what a kiss could feel like. She leaned into Gowan and wished she could melt into him.

Gowan took in a sharp breath and held her at arm's length. "We must stop now. We're tempting fate. We cannae steal what's not ours to have without having to pay it back somehow. I must get you back to your room. First I'll go check the hallway."

Morna didn't want to go, but she nodded, agreeing because he was the only one thinking clearly. Someone had to be strong enough to do what was right. Of course she couldn't stay there in his room. But the thought of never being together was too much to bear. She'd thought that one kiss would quell her heart's longing. Instead, it had set her heart on fire.

He stood at the door and whispered, "It's clear."

Morna went to the door and waited while Gowan checked the hall once again. Then she slipped out and went back to her room.

She'd gotten what she wanted—a kiss to remember.

Chapter Thirteen

Gowan waited outside Morna's bedroom to escort her to breakfast. She opened the door and just smiled. They didn't speak as they made their way down the hall, but as they rounded the corner to go down the stairs, he let his hand brush against hers as if by accident. She took in a sharp breath and lifted her chin but did not turn to look. One kiss had unleashed his heart, and every kiss, every touch, every stolen glance that followed had sealed his fate. All along, they'd been falling and lying to themselves. Now they just had to lie to the world, for they shared something that neither would voice. By not saying the word, they might insulate themselves from the heartache to come.

They sat down to breakfast, and Gowan went through the motions of a life that had utterly changed. He could not look at Morna without feeling the whole world could hear his thoughts. Huntly walked into the room with a vigorous step and grinned at his bride-to-be. He monopolized her attention, talking of plans for the day—a walk first or perhaps a morning ride then a lesson in chess. He loved chess, so she'd have to learn so she could keep up with him.

"I'll try to manage," she said with a feeble attempt at a smile.

Her father asked Huntly if he'd care to go hunting. The two discussed animals and rifles and where they might go that day.

Morna looked at her father and Huntly then lifted bright eyes to meet Gowan's. A blush came to her cheeks, and she quickly looked down.

Gowan wished he hadn't caught her eye and held her gaze. He felt sure no one saw, but at this rate, they would give themselves away.

"You look happy, my dear." Malcolm smiled at his daughter.

Huntly grinned. "'Tis a happy time, is it not?" He reached over and patted Morna's hand.

Her eyes flitted toward him, but unable or unwilling to look at him directly, she picked up her fork and became very focused on eating.

"Ah, that's right, lass. Have a good breakfast, for we'll be hunting today."

She looked genuinely surprised. "I'm afraid I'm not up to hunting today."

Huntly studied her. "Another headache?" He turned to Malcolm. "Has she always been so sickly?"

Malcolm looked taken aback by the comment. "No."

"Dinnae worry about me." She glanced toward the window. "'Tis such a fine day. You won't even miss me."

Huntly's eyes narrowed as he smiled at Morna. "After

we're married, we'll cure those headaches of yours. You do yourself no favors by coddling yourself. If you ask me—"

Morna set her fork down. "But I didn't."

No one spoke for a moment. Morna muttered, "I'm sorry. It's my head. Please, excuse me." She rushed out of the room.

Huntly lifted his eyebrows. Malcolm leaned over to Gowan. "Would you go see what's the matter with her?"

Gowan said, "Aye," as he set down his napkin and fled.

MORNA RAN up the stairs to her room and closed the door. Touching a hand to her burning cheek, she rushed to the window to feel the cool air. She could barely breathe. *How can I marry that man when I can't even make it through breakfast?* No, she was being unkind. It wasn't his fault that she felt something for Gowan. *Something?* She knew what it was. It was love, and she was lost in it. She loved him. *Is that such a terrible thing?* If she was to be married in five days, the answer was yes.

A knock sounded. "Morna."

Morna rushed over and opened the door. "Gowan!"

He caught her wrists before she could fling them about his neck. He cast a nervous glance down the hall. "Have you lost your mind?"

Feeling the sting of rejection, she turned away and whispered, "No, just my heart." Bracing herself for disapproval, she turned back to face him.

"Your father sent me to see what was the matter." Gowan glanced back down the hall then took her hand

and held it in both of his. "Listen to me. We must not give them cause to suspect."

"Aye, you're right! I ken what I must do, but I hate when he talks to me and touches me—like he has the right." She sighed. "And he does. And I hate him—and my father—for that!"

He took a step inside her room and lifted her hand to his lips. "There's naught to be done, so we must find a way to…"

Morna's heart sank. "To what? Endure it? Marry a man I dinnae love, and love a man—" Though she realized what she'd confessed, the damage was done. She quietly finished, but it was no longer a question. "A man I cannae marry." She slipped her hand from his. "Please go." She put her hands on the door to close it, but he gripped the door, holding it open.

He cast another furtive look down the hall and leaned down to say softly but vehemently, "Do you not ken that I love you? I have tried not to say it because it just makes it worse. But I do! And I must sit there politely and watch him regard you like one more possession. And I can do nothing. If I anger the man, I'll lose what little of you I have."

Distant footsteps mounted the stairs. Gowan squeezed her hand and said loudly, "Aye, well, rest and get well, Miss Innes." He gave her one last fervid look then closed the door and headed back down the hall toward the stairs.

Chapter Fourteen

Gowan met Malcolm at the top of the stairs. "Miss Innes sends her apologies. She got another one of her headaches. It's affecting her mood, as you're well aware. She begs your forgiveness for not joining you on the hunt, but she's hoping some rest will restore her good spirits."

Malcolm sighed and shook his head. "Well, I hope she recovers. She's given William a disagreeable impression of her." He lowered his voice and leaned closer. "If she keeps this up, no one would blame him for calling it off."

Gowan tried not to look hopeful. "Could that happen?"

"Perish the thought. William Huntly is a powerful man and a much better friend than an enemy."

With a nod, Gowan said, "I'd best go to him and pass along Miss Innes's apologies."

"Thank you. I'll be down in a few minutes, then we will leave." He started to continue to his room but stopped and turned back. "You'll stay here, of course, to keep an eye on her. When she gets in these moods, she tends to disappear. I cannae have William thinking I cannae keep track of my own daughter, can I?"

"I'll keep her safe while you're gone."

"Good man." He gave Gowan a pat on the back and headed on down the hall to his room.

MORNA SAT in the parlor in one of the cushioned window seats tucked into a handful of dormer windows. Her father and Huntley looked happy enough as they rode away for a morning of hunting. Sighing, she leaned back, but her peace was short-lived as the parlor door opened. She sat up straight but exhaled in relief to see Gowan walk in. He closed the door behind him, strode across the room, and swept Morna into his arms. Her heart leapt as he buried his face in her hair where it fell in cascades on her neck. They had the morning together. Morna breathed in his scent and kissed him again.

Gowan leaned away and smoothed a stray hair from her forehead. He moaned. "Oh, my love. What are we doing?"

"Is it terrible to grasp at one moment of happiness— to have something good to remember?"

His deep gaze was answer enough, but he said the words nonetheless. "I love you. Remember that."

Her mood brightened, and she took his hands in hers. "What if we just ran away?"

Gowan shook his head and sank into the window seat then guided her onto his lap. With his arms circled about her, they looked out through the window at a world that could never be theirs. "If dreams came true, I would do it, but our dream would turn into a nightmare. You've grown up here apart from the world. You dinnae ken what you're asking."

"I'm asking to be with you. I don't care about money."

"That's easy to say when you've always had it. But go a few days without food or shelter, and you'll feel differently."

She leaned her head on his shoulder. "It's easier to go without food than to go without you."

Gowan grinned and gave her a kiss then gazed outside. "The world can be a hard place, my love. I would have you safe at all costs."

"But plenty of people live without money. Your parents did. Why can we not live like that?"

"My parents at least had a home, for a time, anyway. I haven't even got that."

"I dinnae care!"

"But I do. And I'll do what's best for you, whatever it takes."

Morna stood and stared at the gray clouds in the distance. "Even if it means letting Huntly force me into his bed?" When she turned, Gowan was looking down, jaw clenched. She sank into the window seat facing him and leaned her head back. "In five days, I'll be Mrs. William Huntly. My life won't be my own anymore." She gazed at him, but he would not meet her eyes. "How can this be the right thing to do? It's not fair to me. It's not fair to Huntly."

Gowan stared at his hands. "Before I came here, I thought myself a man of honor. I did what was right. If I made mistakes, they were honest and honorable ones. I've never had money, but I was raised to be noble and proud. Now I'm sneaking around in Robert's home—a home his father—your father—accepted me into. He trusts me, and I've stolen your affections from your betrothed—"

"Well, that's just not true."

Gowan leveled an honest look. "And I've lied to conceal it. Have I not stooped low enough?"

Morna folded her arms. "That's a lovely speech, isn't it? And I suppose I had no choice in the matter. My affection is mine, and I gave it to you. My father may be able to bargain my body away to the highest bidder, but Huntly will never have my heart."

All hope was gone from Gowan's eyes. "We cannae run from the truth. We have nothing between us—no money or hope for the future—only love. And that isnae enough."

He stood and pulled Morna into his arms. Then he kissed her until nothing else mattered—no future, no wedding, just Gowan and love and two hearts slowly breaking.

The door opened, and he nearly leapt from the window alcove and leaned casually against the wall while Morna grabbed a book and buried her nose in it.

In walked a scullery maid. "Och! You gave me a fright. I didnae see you two there!" She proceeded to tend to the fire while Gowan and Morna held their poses in silence.

When she'd finally gone, Morna put her hand on her chest. "*We* gave *her* a fright? My heart is still pounding!"

Staring at the door, Gowan said, "We cannae live like this—taking risks."

Morna offered no argument. Their near miss was proof of how easily they could be found out. They'd managed to dodge the notice of the scullery maid, but next time, they might not be so lucky.

After heaving a sigh, she said, "Five days from now, I'm to stand before God and vow to forsake all others when in my heart I cannot. And I will vow to love a man I will not ever love. I will have to pretend I do not love another. Risk or no risk, it will still be a lie."

Gowan said nothing.

A long silence followed, then Morna said, "Either way, I will be living that lie—even if I never saw you again."

Gowan sat down facing her and took her hands in his. "And either way, I will love you."

"Is that to be my comfort? To know love but not feel its touch?"

Gowan nodded and stared at her hands. "I should go."

She flashed a panicked look at him. "Go... to your room? Or leave forever?"

"I promised your brother to take care of you, but how could he have envisioned this? Of course he did not, for he trusted me not to fall in love with his sister." He let go of her hands and leaned back with self-loathing.

"Or maybe he thought that we might fall in love, giving me one small bit of happiness to treasure forever."

"I must go. It's the best thing for both of us."

She wanted to cry out or beg, but instead she softly said, "No."

"I'll stay until the wedding is over. After that, I'll make up a story—a family member who needs me. I'll slip away quietly, and no one will ever know about us."

Morna wanted to cry out, to beg, or to argue why he shouldn't go. But she knew he was right.

They sat in silent despair until Morna could no longer feel even that. She was numb. Quietly, she said, "I have one thing to ask."

Gowan fixed questioning eyes on her.

She said, "Lie with me."

Gowan looked stunned. When he'd recovered, he shook his head. "Lass..."

"Huntly cannae be my first. Please?"

With a pained look, he got up and stepped away, turning his back to her as if even a look would consume them with fire. "You asked for a kiss, and God help me, I gave it to you. And now this. If we were caught..."

Morna stood. "Just once."

He didn't answer. Apparently, he could not even bring himself to look at her.

So she said, "Come to my room." And she left.

At least she had asked. That was one less regret she'd have to live with.

MORNA PACED BACK and forth in front of her bedchamber fireplace with a feeling of dread in the pit of her stomach. He wasn't coming. He hadn't said no, but he hadn't said yes. How like Gowan, always doing what was right.

She used to try to be honest and do the right thing, but she'd never known love was so strong she'd be willing to throw everything she believed out the window. But she wanted to know real love so she'd have something to cling to on those lonely nights of marriage that loomed before her. If that was selfish, so be it.

A small tap came at the door, and she ran over and flung it open. Gowan rushed in, and Morna closed the door and locked it.

His gaze burned as he shook his head. He had changed his mind.

"It can only be once."

Morna gave a weak nod, then he took her face in his hands and kissed her fiercely until she felt light-headed.

Gowan looked into her eyes. "You asked this of me, so now I have something to ask of you. Remember that I love you. For from now on, no matter where I am or what happens, I'll not take a breath without longing for you."

He scooped her up into his arms and carried her to the bed.

Chapter Fifteen

Whether an hour or two had passed, Morna did not know or care. She lay in Gowan's arms, stretched against the length of his body, bare skin against bare skin. Life would never feel the same again. Still feeling his ragged breath on her neck, she remembered the passion between them. She would ache to be with him like this, but she would not think of that now. She would savor the moment and breathe in his scent like the fresh Highland air she so loved, and she'd smile to feel the weight of his arm across her chest. She was drowsy from love, but she would not fall asleep.

Gowan murmured, "What?"

"I didnae say anything."

He propped his head on his hand, ran his fingertip around the outline of her lips, then slowly swept his eyes up to hers. "I dinnae ken what I loved first about you." His eyes twinkled. "Was it your blade in my neck? No... I think it was when I sat beside you at our first supper, and you didnae speak to me throughout the whole meal."

"It's not that I wouldn't." She shrugged. "I had nothing to say."

He rolled over and landed on top of her, grinning. "Oh, aye? And what have you to say now?"

She smiled, but it faded. "That I love you."

A warm glow came into his eyes. "Oh, my love." He kissed her and set about once more showing her how much he loved her.

A thunderclap shook the window, and they flinched then laughed about it.

Then Gowan froze. "A thunderstorm. Good God, how long has it been raining?"

Morna wrinkled her brow. "I dinnae ken. I've been too busy to care." She smiled softly.

"If it's storming, they might come home." With one last kiss, he said, "I must go."

In the midst of that kiss, a key turned in the latch, and the door opened. Gowan rolled off of Morna and froze while Morna pulled the bedding up to her neck.

The housekeeper's eyes opened wide. "My laird, they're in here."

Malcolm stepped into the doorway. "Stay back, William. You've no need to see this." He locked enraged eyes on Gowan then tore them away to eye his daughter with contempt.

Despite Malcolm's efforts to restrain him, Huntly pushed his way into the doorway. His face showed no emotion as he quietly said, "Your daughter's personal guard appears to enjoy his work." He turned to Malcolm. "The wedding is off." His bootsteps echoed as he strode down the hall.

Malcolm said, "Put your clothes on. Gowan, meet me

in my study. Morna, I'll send for you later." He turned to the housekeeper. "After they take Dunbar, lock the door."

"Yes, sir."

He gave a nod in the other direction, and two guards stepped into view and stood shoulder to shoulder across from the door.

The housekeeper put her hand on the door handle and said sternly, "You have one minute to get dressed." Then she pulled the door closed.

Gowan gripped Morna's shoulders. "I love you." He clutched her to him then leapt out of bed and hastily dressed.

Morna dressed almost as quickly and rushed over to him. "Will I see you again?"

"Och, lass." He looked deep into her eyes then suddenly kissed her with what felt like all the passion a heart could hold. As quickly as it had begun, the kiss was over, and Gowan was on his way to the door. With one dark look back, he turned and left.

The key turned in the lock.

A GUARD on each side had viselike grips on his arms as they walked Gowan to the study. Once there, they released him and stood by the door.

"Come here," Malcolm said gruffly from the opposite side of the room.

Gowan complied. He said nothing, for even before seeing Malcolm's expression, he knew there was no point in making excuses. He'd do better to face the consequences, whatever they might be.

Malcolm stood on the other side of the large desk and glared at Gowan. "I brought you into my house, into my son Robert's room, and I treated you like family. In turn, you brought an end to a wedding that would have benefitted everyone involved. You... defiled my daughter. I could kill you right now, and no one would miss you."

Gowan felt every muscle and nerve tense. His thoughts raced with heightened awareness just as he used to feel while in battle. He knew every exit and every item within reach that he could use as a weapon, and he sized up his opponent. Malcolm was shorter but broader of shoulder. But Gowan was younger and stronger.

Looking Malcolm straight in the eye, Gowan said, "God help me, I love her."

Malcolm stared back with little reaction, save the barely perceptible narrowing of his eyes. He slowly walked around to the front of his desk then struck Gowan's face with the back of his hand. "Get him out of my sight."

Gowan's mind raced with the best way to proceed. He had two ways out: through the windows and down several stories to certain death or through two husky guards between him and the door. No, he would wait until he was out of the room, where the chance for escape would be better. He could flee and plan a way to come back for Morna, for he feared what Malcolm might do.

He made a last-ditch attempt to reason with Malcolm. "I want to marry her. I—"

Before he could finish, something struck him on the back of his head, and the meeting was over.

MORNA SAT STARING at the fire, awaiting her summons to her father's study and wondering why it was taking so long. She got up and paced, then a knock at last sounded. The key turned in the lock, and to her surprise, her father walked in. She'd expected the housekeeper or anyone else to take her to him.

Malcolm planted himself in front of the door.

"Father, I love him! I'm sorry. I ken that you wanted this wedding, but I dinnae love William Huntly, and I never will. Gowan and I are in love!"

"Love is for poets. You've thrown away an advantageous alliance that would have secured your future."

"And yours." What she'd intended as an accusation came out sounding like a weak afterthought.

Her father ignored the remark and continued. "But you were too stubborn to do what I asked, and now it's too late. You've lost your fine husband and home, and you've ruined your life."

"Gowan will marry me. He's all that I need."

"Och! A kiss and a drink of water make a poor breakfast. What sort of life did you think you would have? He cannae provide for you, and you'd be a burden to him. Before long, you'd wind up in the poorhouse. And do you ken what they do with women who are a drain on the parish coffers, husband or not? They sell them."

"No! That's absurd!"

"Oh, aye. Dinnae look so shocked. There's a world out there I've sheltered you from. You'll wish you'd married Huntly."

Morna didn't know what to say. No matter what she did, she was powerless to determine her own fate. Still, she had faith in Gowan. He would never let such a thing happen to her.

Malcolm grew quiet. "I'll not subject you to that fate. But for your protection, this room will be your home now, and it will remain locked."

"You'd make me a prisoner?"

"Better here than the poorhouse."

Morna looked straight at him, but he would not meet her eyes. "Until when?"

"Until I let you out."

"You wouldn't! Father, no!"

He left and closed the door behind him.

Morna rushed to the door and slammed her hand against it. "Father!"

The key turned in the lock.

She had to get out. She didn't know where Gowan was or where she would go, but she *had* to get out.

Pacing in front of the windows, Morna tried to figure out a plan. Her father was a methodical man. He valued routine. Of course he would put Gowan in the dungeon. Perhaps she could get someone to tell her his whereabouts when they brought her supper. But knowing was of no use if she couldn't get to him. If her brother were alive, he would know what to do. She whispered, "He's locked me away. Robert, what do I do?"

Suddenly, she stopped, and her eyes opened wide. "We had keys!"

She went to her writing desk and pulled one of the drawers all the way out. In the very back was a false back a couple of inches from the real back, creating a hidden compartment. Morna had forgotten about it until that moment.

She and Robert had found it when they were children. One day, when Morna was seven and Robert twelve, they were playing at spies when they found important enemy stores of biscuits in the pantry. They were munching on their spoils when they spotted the housekeeper's keys on the table. She'd unwittingly set them down and left the room. Knowing it wouldn't be long before she discovered them missing and returned, Robert and Morna decided to make impressions of their bedroom keys. Weeks before, Robert had been punished by being locked in his room, so the idea of making their own keys was irresistible. He quickly grabbed a candle from the box on the shelf and warmed it by the fire enough to press the key into the wax, first one side, then the other. They were just about to repeat the process with the other key when they heard the housekeeper approaching. Someone stopped her to talk, so they quickly made an impression of the second key while the housekeeper's footsteps drew closer. She came into the kitchen just as the outside door quietly closed.

Days later, after setting their key project aside for lack of supplies, they spied a gardener repairing the roof of the gardening shed with some tin flashing. Pretending to be spies, they waited and watched.

Morna grew weary of their game, but Robert insisted. "Och, Morna, he'll need a break soon."

Morna sighed, and they waited.

Minutes later, they ran up the stairs and into Robert's room, laughing and gasping for air with lead flashing and wire cutters from the gardener's toolbox. By the end of the afternoon, they each had a spare key to their bedrooms.

Morna smiled to recall her childhood adventures with Robert. She sighed. *Why did everything have to change?*

Before he left, Robert had said, "If anything happens to me, it won't do to have you moping around here. I won't have it."

"Dinnae flatter yourself, Robert Innes." She grinned, but as she said it, a dark mood came over her. She gave him a hug to hide it, but somehow in that moment she felt his absence as if it were already happening. The feeling passed quickly, yet somehow she could not shake the feeling that he was leaving forever.

With a deep breath, she set her emotions aside, reached into the hidden drawer, and pulled out her home-made key. She wanted to test it, but it was too soft. She feared it might break. As it was, she remembered having to use a hatpin pressed against it for support to get it to work properly. She reached into the drawer once more and smiled. There it was. Key and hatpin in hand, she was ready to make her escape. *But to where?*

She sat down on her bed and lifted the linen. It still smelled like Gowan. When she shut her eyes, she could almost feel him.

Clutching his pillow to her chest, Morna lay down. She had to focus on forming a plan. If she tried to leave now, too many servants might see her. Then a question formed in her mind. *How did Father find out?* He had come prepared with a housekeeper and two guards—and Huntly, of course. Someone had to have told him. But who? No one had seen them together.

Except for the scullery maid.

Morna sat up, still clutching the pillow. The maid must have suspected. *Dear God, did she follow us to the bedroom?* She must have suspected and told her father and Huntly as soon as they walked in the door.

In spite of it all, Morna had been relieved when Huntly called off the wedding. For one moment, she'd actually thought true love might be enough to sway her father. Once he saw how true their love was, he'd understand that she and Gowan belonged together. She shut her eyes and took a deep breath. Instead, he'd locked her in her room.

Morna opened the window and breathed in the cool air, hoping it might clear her head. What she needed to do was to think of the future. She needed a plan. She couldn't risk being seen, for she'd only have one chance. She would have to be patient and wait until dark. Then she would steal away and find Gowan.

They would be together.

Chapter Sixteen

Morna thought she'd go mad waiting. At last, she was preparing to leave when the scullery maid brought her supper. Morna wanted to ask about Gowan's whereabouts, but it was pointless. She would only report back to her father and raise further suspicion. Instead, Morna silently waited until the maid left the room. Morna sighed with dismay. Now she was forced to delay her escape until the maid returned to retrieve the empty tray. *What if she doesn't return? What if she leaves it here until morning?* Morna decided to wait for the moon to rise high in the sky. If the scullery maid hadn't come for the tray by that time, Morna would leave.

The moon rose, and Morna pressed her ear to the door. The castle was quiet, so she slipped the key into the lock with the hatpin for support. It didn't work. Morna tried it again, and a third time. She started to panic. She had no other plan. She took a moment to pull herself together then tried the key again. This time, it worked.

She made her way down the hallway and down the

back staircase. The kitchen was dark. Pausing at the door, Morna glanced toward the pantry. After a quick detour to the silver, she put a handful in each pocket then slipped out through the kitchen door. Her heart hammered as she stood in the shadows beside the stone wall. Working her way along the edge of the wall, she forced herself not to nervously rush lest she make too much noise and miss seeing or hearing someone approaching. It was only a two- or three-minute walk to the dungeon, but tonight, it felt so much longer.

At last, she arrived. No guard was on duty. That seemed strange. Something wasn't right. She hid and looked to make sure the guard wasn't concealed by shadows. Convinced he would be gone for a minute or two, Morna dared to go closer. This was the part that could be her undoing.

"Psst!" She waited then whispered, "Gowan." In one last attempt, she crept to the bars and grabbed hold as she peered inside, but the door swung open. The cell was empty. She carefully closed it then ran to the dark shadows under a tree to hide while she decided what to do next.

Hours earlier

Gowan awoke in the dungeon with an ache in his head to rival any he'd suffered in battle. He reached up and winced. Memories came back in hazy images. He'd been struck. He sat up and looked around. It was still daylight, so he couldn't have been unconscious for long. He tried to imagine what the laird had in mind. If

Malcolm had wanted to kill him, surely he'd have done it by now... unless he was planning to wait until dark.

And what of Morna? The Highlands were full of tales of young women falling in love with the wrong men. They never ended well. Gowan blamed himself for what had happened. He'd known better than to succumb to temptation. But this was more than a passing temptation —it was love. And Gowan was no match for its power. He would pay the price, but Morna did not deserve anything her father might have in store for her. Leaning back against the rough stone wall, he closed his eyes and let the pain and self-loathing wash over him.

He'd been dozing but awoke to the sound of approaching footsteps. It was dark, so he could have been sleeping for hours. Malcolm rounded the corner with the same two guards as before close behind him. Gowan stood to face Malcolm as he stopped in front of the barred cell door.

"In the letter you brought from my son, Robert wrote that you'd saved his life. For that reason alone, I have decided to spare yours. But it isnae my first choice."

The laird paused as if he expected him to grovel and thank him. But Gowan could muster little remorse when he loved Morna so deeply. *How can he not see this?* Granted, Gowan came from humble crofters, but marriage to Huntly would have made Morna profoundly unhappy. *What kind of father would do that to a child?* No, Gowan would not thank him. He would stand before him in a silent show of respect, which was as much as Gowan could manage at the moment.

"My guards will escort you to Aberdeen. There you will board the next ship out of Scotland.

"I will not!"

"But you will. One way or the other."

Gowan shook his head. "My laird, do you not remember being in love?"

Malcolm's face clouded. "I remember inviting you into my house so you could betray my trust by bedding my daughter." He turned, gave a nod to his guards, and walked away.

The guards opened the door to the cell and tied his hands behind his back.

"Any trouble, and we'll have no choice but to kill you. Nothing personal, you ken. But we'll do what we must."

There was a problem with one of the horses. While the guards disagreed over which horse to take instead, Gowan seized the moment. Hoping Morna would question the boy, he casually leaned over to Sionn and grinned. "They'd best decide, or I'll miss the next ship out of Aberdeen."

The boy smiled and finished saddling the horses. Minutes later, they were on the road for Aberdeen, with Gowan's hands still tied behind his back and his horse tethered to one of the guard's horses.

THEY ARRIVED IN ABERDEEN, where the next ship wasn't leaving until morning. The guards secured a room in a dockside inn, tied Gowan's hands and feet to the bedpost at the foot of the bed, then went downstairs to the tavern for some ale and supper. Every few minutes, one of the guards came up to check on him, but they needn't have bothered. They tied knots like sailors.

How fitting, Gowan thought between curses, considering where he was going.

By morning, Gowan was pondering the various ways he might escape from the ship while in dock when the guards awoke.

The taller one stood and went to the window while the other sat on the edge of the bed, looking groggy. "Och, Duff, my head hurts."

"Aye, I ken how you feel," Gowan said wryly. Still aching from being struck on the head, he was in no humor to suffer their sorry complaints. They'd had a soft bed to sleep on, while Gowan had spent the night on the hard wooden floor.

"So, lads, can you tell me what's happened to Morna?" Getting no response, he shrugged. "I'm too far away to cause trouble."

"She's locked up. That's all you need to know." Duff turned from the window and went to the door.

"In the dungeon?" Gowan probed, hoping they'd let down their defenses in their hungover state.

Duff shrugged. "That's the least of your worries."

Gowan said, "I've been to sea. 'Tis no bother. So where am I off to?"

The two guards exchanged glances, then Duff said, "Och, we wouldnae want to spoil the surprise." He turned to the other guard. "Walrick, watch him, I'll go get us some breakfast." And he left.

Chapter Seventeen

Morna had no place to hide in the nearly treeless slopes that surrounded the castle. She'd be caught before noon if she ventured on foot. But sneaking a horse out of the stable would be no easy task either. Young Sionn lay on a bed of hay near the first stall. She would have to get past him not once but twice, the second time with a horse. When she took a step forward, the boy stirred and rolled over. She looked upward and shook her head. What made her think she could escape, she wasn't quite sure. It was more of a question of choices, and she only had one.

She tiptoed to the stall and put her hand on the door.

"Miss Innes?" Sionn looked up at her with round eyes. "They said you were locked in your room."

She put a finger to her lips. "Aye, lad. I'm out now, and I must go see Mr. Dunbar."

He glanced nervously toward the opposite side of the stable then shook his head at her. "He's gone, miss."

"I know. And if I'm to go see him, I'll need a horse."

"Och, if I let you do that, the head groom will have my hide."

She took his chin in her hand and looked softly at him. "I'll not do that to you. But what if I came in here and forced you?"

Grinning, he said, "Och, miss, you wouldnae do that."

She smiled. "But if you told the head groom that I had, he couldnae be angry with you."

"No, I suppose not."

"So... would you do that for me?"

His eyebrows drew together. "I dinnae ken. It would be a lie."

"It's all right, lad." She turned to leave.

"All right, miss. Mr. Dunbar has been kind to me, and I hate to think of him on that ship."

"Ship?"

"Aye, the guards argued 'bout which horse to take 'cause the horse they wanted to take threw a shoe. And we needed a shoe from the blacksmith. But he's away to Inverness for his uncle's funeral, and—"

"Sionn. Which ship?"

"Mr. Dunbar said if they didnae hurry, he'd miss the next ship out of Aberdeen."

"Mr. Dunbar said that to you?"

"Aye."

She took Sionn's face in her hands and kissed him on the forehead. "Thank you, Sionn!"

He looked at her with a puzzled expression while she went into the nearest stall and saddled the horse. With Sionn's help, it was only a few minutes later that she stood in the doorway, holding the reins.

"Wait until you see the first light of dawn, then go tell the head groom I forced my way into the stall, and you couldn't stop me."

"Aye, miss. Goodbye." He gave her a bashful but adoring smile.

"Goodbye, sweet lad." She smiled and touched his cheek then rode out into the night.

MORNA SAT up with a jerk and realized she had fallen asleep in the saddle, and her horse had veered off for a drink in a stream. She dismounted and went to the edge of the water. While her horse rested and drank, she splashed a few handfuls of water on her face then looked about for signs of the road. To her good fortune, the horse had trampled a trail through the grass, so she was not as lost as she feared.

She made it back onto the road and into Aberdeen and found her way to the Trinity Quay. There she stabled her horse then went in search of the next ship out of port. The silver in her pockets clinked when she walked, so she walked with care so as not to call attention to it. After asking around, she learned that a boat would be leaving for the colonies, so she went to the ship and approached some sailors standing nearby for more information.

Her first attempts to gain information failed because the sailors were more interested in her than the ship, but Morna managed to glean from one sailor with whisky-scented breath that the ship sailed at dawn.

His eyes glimmered as he said, "No one has boarded her yet except crew, but I'll let you board her if you let me board you." He grinned and put his arm around her, but as he drew closer, the sharp point of her sgian-dubh was waiting for his ribcage. He suddenly changed his mind and walked away grumbling.

ON THE WAY TO ABERDEEN, Gowan had had no food and only water to drink, provided he knelt down, hands tied behind his back, and drank it from streams with the horses. So when Duff returned from downstairs with a tray, Gowan's mouth watered at the sight and scent of eggs and freshly baked bread. Duff handed a plate to Walrick, who'd remained behind with Gowan, then he set down a plate and a half-pint of ale before Gowan. He even untied his hands. Gowan ate, knowing that it would be the last good thing he'd have to eat until landing... wherever that turned out to be.

While eating, he kept an eye on the others for any chance to fight them off and escape. He had no utensils to eat with, and the half-pint pewter mug lacked the weight to do very much damage. Having to sit on the floor put him at a disadvantage. The split second it would take him to stand would give them a chance to react before he even got close enough to land the first punch. So he watched and waited for an opportunity. If none came, he would wait until a guard came close enough to kick his feet out from under him, then he'd go after the other before the first could get back on his feet. Two against one were not his favorite odds, but he'd had worse to contend with in battle, and he'd survived. So this was his best path to freedom.

They finished eating, and Gowan was ready. Duff eyed him. "Are you ready to go?"

That struck him as odd. For the entire length of their journey, he had shown no concern for Gowan. But he forgot about that as his vision grew blurry. Gowan lifted his eyebrows then squinted, unable to focus.

Duff drew his dirk and said, "Get up and put your hands behind your back."

He stood, but the room teetered, and Gowan's head tilted with it. Unable to find solid ground to plant his feet on, he stumbled. The guards stood on either side of him, pulling Gowan's arms over their shoulders.

Gowan lifted his head, barely able to speak. "Bastard."

Walrick stumbled and fell on the bed with a moan.

Duff cursed and muttered, "Och, the stupid wench must have put it in both of their drinks."

The rest was a blur. He was vaguely aware of being dragged down the stairs and out to the docks. In the back of his semiconscious mind, Gowan knew that he didn't want to go, but when he tried to fight back, his body refused to cooperate. There were gaps where he lost consciousness and would seem to awake shortly after. He heard voices and saw a large ship, but none of it made any sense.

Someone cried out a curse, and Gowan slumped over.

Chapter Eighteen

Morna waited for over an hour by the dock, pacing back and forth in front of the next ship set to sail. The last bits of cargo were loaded, and the last of the crew boarded the vessel. Losing heart, Morna dug down deep and clung to hope. Gowan's life might depend upon her. She would not let him down.

Sailors hoisted the gangplank. The ship was about to set sail. Morna knew this might happen. If this ship wasn't the one Gowan was to sail on, she would wait at the next, and the next after that until she found him.

She turned and glanced down the quay. A pair of urchins ran about playing and jostled some people. Poor lads... life was hard with no money. Unable to determine which ship would be next to set sail, Morna decided to go to a tavern for breakfast and ask around there. First, she would need to cash in the silver she'd brought. She felt certain what she'd brought would last several months. She touched her pockets. The clink of silver brought the comfort of knowing she had the means to survive, no matter what happened. There, in two pockets tied about her waist and safely hidden between layers of skirts lay her means of support.

Morna continued to scan the dockside, looking for Gowan. Amongst the growing number of sailors, tradesmen, and travelers, two men emerged from an inn. They drew her notice because one man was clearly the worse for wear, not having slept off his drink. She'd had enough dealings with sailors this morning to feel sure this was not an unusual occurrence. From the looks of it, they were making their way through the crowd toward one of the ships on the dock. She didn't envy any man setting sail on the rough North Sea in such a condition, but he'd brought it on himself. He'd get no sympathy from her. Were it not for the help of the man beside him, who was practically carrying him along, she had no doubt he'd still be slumped over a table in a dark, smoky corner of the pub.

Shaking her head, she began to look back to the ship when she happened to get a closer view of the man. From the clothing alone, it might have been Gowan, and the hair color and build were the same. But it couldn't be Gowan. He was not prone to heavy drinking, and Sionn had told her two guards would be with him. Yet she could not look away. There was something about him. If only his head weren't slumped over. She had to get a better look to be sure.

She drew closer but still couldn't get a good look at his face. Only a few feet away, she glanced up at his friend and gasped. He'd drawn his bluebonnets over his forehead, but when he looked at her, she recognized him as one of her father's men. At the same moment, he recognized her and put his hand on the hilt of a dirk sheathed at his side.

Time seemed to slow down as she tried to think of the best course of action. Gowan was not himself, so she would be on her own. Robert had taught her to fight, but this man was even taller than Gowan. Moreover, her small sgian-dubh was no match for his dirk. Since he worked for her father and knew who she was, she was sure he would take care not to hurt her, but she had no such confidence where Gowan was concerned. She had to do something that would not risk his life.

She called out, "Gowan!"

Gowan looked up, bewildered, and slowly blinked. "Morna?"

She shouted, "Get down!"

Not only Gowan but several passersby also ducked down when they heard her, and one frail elderly woman lost her balance and fell.

Seeing this, Morna pointed at Duff and yelled, "That man struck that poor woman! Someone stop him!"

Duff shouted a curse as three men wrestled him to the ground. Morna hoped someone would help the old woman, because she had her eyes on Gowan. As a commotion ensued a few feet away, Morna knelt down and gripped Gowan's arm.

"Gowan, listen to me. You've got to get up. I can't do this alone. You've got to get up and walk."

She tugged, and he tried and stumbled.

"Are you all right, miss?"

She looked up to find a well-dressed gentleman peering down at her. "Not really. It's my husband."

"Too much to drink?"

With round, pitiful eyes, she said, "If I can just get him back to the farm. The children and I need him."

"Of course, madam. Have you a carriage?"

"Just a horse, I'm afraid."

He shook his head and cast a dark eye on Gowan then said, "Which stable?"

"It's not far, just over there."

The gentleman helped pull Gowan to his feet, then he and Morna managed to get Gowan to the stable, where he hoisted Gowan sideways over the saddle.

Morna thanked the gentleman and watched him leave, then she turned back to the stableman, who was waiting to be paid.

She winced when she realized that she had not yet exchanged her silver for money. With Gowan as he was, going anywhere now would be out of the question. So she decided to offer a small silver fork or spoon. She cringed, knowing its value was far more than she owed, but it was worth it to get Gowan to safety.

"I'm sorry. I haven't got any money with me, but this piece of silver should more than cover it. If you'll excuse me a moment." She went around the corner of a stall to discreetly retrieve the silver from the pocket hidden under the top layer of skirts, but the familiar weight of the silver was gone. Trying to hide her panic, she patted her skirts, desperately searching for the missing silver. Then she found the cut end of a pocket string. She felt for the other one. It was cut too. "My pockets." She looked at the stableman in disbelief. "They're gone."

The stableman said, "Pickpockets. Oh, aye. It's terrible the way they prey on innocent people like that."

"But my pockets were under my skirt. They couldn't get to them."

"Och, 'tis a common trick—cutting the string. Down goes the pocket. You're never the wiser. They train children to do it. They're small. People tend not to notice them."

Morna grimaced. "But I would've felt all that silver fall, and the loss of its weight." She shut her eyes and exhaled as she recalled the young urchins at play. "The crowd."

"Aye, crowds are best for that line of work."

During all the commotion she'd caused, all Morna had cared about was getting Gowan to safety. At least she'd done that.

The stableman shook his head. "I'm sorry, but you'll still have to pay, or I cannae let you take that horse."

Morna looked over at Gowan, who was helplessly slumped over the horse. "But I've no money, and I cannae just leave him here."

"Och, no, you're right there. This isnae an inn."

Dismayed, Morna thought for a moment. Perhaps she could do a day's work for the money she owed. "Do you know where I can find work?"

He eyed her up and down. "You might ask in the pubs and inns, but the kind of work you'll find there might not be the kind of work you want."

With a slow nod, she turned to slide Gowan off the saddle. She managed to get his arms over her shoulders before he slumped down. He moaned as she inched him toward the road.

The stableman called out, "There's always the poorhouse if it comes to that."

Appalled, Morna said, "A poorhouse? No, I don't think that will be necessary."

"Oh, aye. Well, if you get hungry enough, 'tis good to know. Just head over to Union Street and ask around. Most folk ken where it is."

With that thought, too disturbing to contemplate, Morna offered the man a weak thank-you, took a firm grip of the wrist hanging over her shoulder, and coaxed Gowan along down the street.

He was growing a bit more responsive to Morna's instructions, managing not only to stay upright but also to shuffle his feet forward. But they had nowhere to go, and Walrick and Duff would be searching for them. If they caught up with Morna and Gowan, they would be unable to escape, for Gowan was in no condition to do anything but sleep it off. *But where?*

With no money, no horse, and no shelter, she wasn't sure where they could go. She stopped in front of a wynd and heaved a weary sigh. "Has it come to this?"

As if answering, Gowan grunted then rested his head on her shoulder and felt increasingly heavy. Then he started to snore.

"Oh no, not here." She turned and headed down the wynd. "Almost there. Just a few more steps."

When they got to the end of the wynd, Morna eased Gowan down to the ground in a shadowy corner to sleep off whatever they'd drugged him with. Having ridden all night, Morna felt exhausted, so she curled up beside Gowan and covered them both with the end of his plaid, and they drifted to sleep.

Chapter Nineteen

Gowan awoke to the warm softness of a woman in his arms and the cold hard ground beneath him. He snuggled against her and moaned as he brushed his lips over her neck and shoulder. "Och, my head's achin'."

She rolled over to face him and leaned into his chest. "Gowan! Thank God you're back!"

"Back from where? And where are we?"

"Aberdeen."

He shook his head, trying to clear the clouded memories of the past day. "My head's mince. How did you get here?"

"No time for that story. You were drugged, and my father's guards are searching for you."

"Aye, I remember the trip here. And you got away?"

Morna shrugged and looked at him with twinkling eyes.

"Och, lass, you're a wonder."

"No, I'm just in love—or off my head." A smile bloomed on her face.

Gowan kissed her and held her, then he buried his face in the crook of her neck and whispered into her ear, "This is not as soft as your bed, but I think we could manage." He grinned and ran his palms over her satiny skin. "My God, you're here, and you're so beautiful. Ow!"

Someone had kicked him in the side. He rolled over and instinctively reached for his dirk, but the guards had taken it from him. At the same time, Morna reached for her sgian-dubh.

But strong hands grabbed her arms from behind, pulled her to her feet, and relieved her of the knife. "I'll take that, madam."

Gowan started to swing his fist, but the one holding Morna said, "I wouldnae do that."

In the dark, he could not see their expressions to gauge their intentions or how well they were armed. Had he been alone, he'd have risked fighting back, but with Morna there, he would not take the risk. He lifted his hands. Once more, he found himself with his hands tied behind his back, but the voices were not those of Walrick or Duff.

"Come along," said one.

"Where?" Gowan asked. "And if you don't mind my asking, what have we done?"

"We dinnae allow vagrants to sleep on the street."

They arrived at the street, where streetlights revealed their captors to be two police constables.

Gowan protested, "We're no vagrants."

"Oh, aye, I can see that," one constable said, unimpressed.

Morna said, "We were robbed. Pickpockets stole my silver."

The other constable said, "The same thing happened to me. When I left home this morning, I had a pot full of gold. Now it's gone, so I have to work for a living, getting the likes of you off the streets."

Morna's jaw dropped, indignant fury in her eyes. "The likes of us? I'll have you know my father's a wealthy landowner. He lives near Inverness."

Her constable laughed. "And my father's the king of England. He lives in London."

Trying to sound calm, Gowan said, "We're not beggars. We just have no money."

"Not beggars, just poor?"

Gowan exhaled. "At the moment, but—"

"Good. We've got just the place for you. A warm bed and a hot meal and you'll be as good as new."

The constables tugged them along down the street.

MINUTES LATER, they stopped in front of a gate in the midst of a wall that stretched from one street to the next. Above the gate was a sign.

Morna gasped. "The poorhouse? No! We dinnae belong here."

Gowan pulled back, resisting the constable. "Now just hold on. You're making a mistake."

"Aye, we hear that a lot. Come along."

Gowan complied, but as they approached the front gate, he broke free and fought off the constable, striking a blow that sent him to the ground. Morna struggled but could not free herself from the firm clutches of the other constable. He forced her through the gate, where he handed her off to the gatekeeper. Then he went back to help his fellow constable.

Morna was whisked away, crying, "Get away, Gowan!"

While he fended off the two constables, the gate closed between them, and Morna disappeared behind the large wooden doors of the building.

The two constables finally managed to pin Gowan down to the ground. "Now you've bought yourself a nice jail cell. Your new roommates might not be as bonnie as your last, but we hope you'll find it to your liking."

While they laughed, thoughts raced through Gowan's mind. He would be no help to Morna in jail, so he had to get free for her sake. With renewed strength of purpose, Gowan rammed his head into one laughing man's face, struck a sharp blow with his elbow into the other one's neck, then ran. It took them a few seconds to recover before they made chase, giving Gowan a valuable head start of several seconds. They chased him down the street and around the corner, but Gowan outran them and disappeared into Aberdeen's shadowy closes and wynds.

MORNA WAS TAKEN into a women's ward, where she was stripped down, bathed, and given new clothes. From there, a matron took her to a new room. As they walked, the matron said, "Everyone here has to work."

"What sort of work?" Morna asked.

"The men usually break piles of stones, and the women pick oakum. But we're out at the moment, so you're lucky. You'll get to spend your days knitting."

Morna closed her eyes for a moment. *Knitting?*

"Here." The matron handed her a ball of yarn and two knitting needles.

Morna eyed them with reluctance.

"Well, come on, lass. Get to work." The woman was all business and lacking in patience. With a stern look, she said, "You're not going to be a troublemaker, are you?"

Taking the yarn and needles, Morna replied, "No."

"There's a good lass."

Morna sat down and looked at the needles. "What do I knit?"

"Scarves, hats, and mittens. Winter's coming. If you need help, ask the others. Go on."

Morna did as instructed and remained there for the rest of the day, knitting something that didn't quite look like a scarf, hat, or mitten. But they were the ones who had asked her to knit, so they could take what they got. Of course, they'd have to figure out what that was because, so far, it looked like something a cat had coughed up.

How can I concentrate on knitting when Gowan is out there in Aberdeen somewhere? She was safe enough, she supposed, but she was worried about Gowan.

MORNA NEED NOT HAVE WONDERED, for as Gowan ran down a close and rounded the corner, he ran into another constable. Trapped in an alley between two constables, he had no place to go. Instead of the jail he'd expected, the poorhouse was closer, so they decided to walk him back there and be rid of him. Now he would be closer to Morna.

Once inside the poorhouse, he was told he would stay

two nights and complete one full day of work in between, after which he would be released. He was taken into a room where a porter was in charge of lining the men up to take turns bathing in a tub. They all shared the same water, and Gowan was at the end of the line. Once bathed, he was given clean clothes. His were taken to be washed. They told him they'd be returned when he left. He was then given his supper, which consisted of eight ounces of bread and a pint of gruel.

The next morning, Gowan woke to a bell rung by the porter. He bathed and dressed, ate a breakfast of leftover gruel and a small piece of bread, then went to the main hall for the weekly prayer service led by the head of the poorhouse. Gowan searched the crowd of a hundred or so and finally found Morna, but she didn't see him. Not knowing Gowan was there, she would have had no reason to look for him.

After prayer time, the women and men were lined up to go to their separate work areas and would not be together again for the rest of the week. As Morna reached the doorway, Gowan called her name then avoided the ire of the porter by innocently staring into the distance as though someone else had caused the disruption. Morna's head turned, and her eyes met his. He exhaled, contented. She knew he was there.

Gowan spent his day in the laundry, had a dinner break at one o'clock, and had supper at six. The next morning, the bell woke him again. Those who were leaving were ushered into a room, where they received their own clothes to change into. Then they were released to the long walk that led to the gate, but he lingered, looking for Morna.

The porter approached. "Are you staying or going?"

Gowan didn't want to take his eyes from the exit. If Morna wasn't coming out, he needed to stay inside with her, but the porter gave him a nudge. "Go on!"

"I can't. I'm waiting for someone."

"Go wait by the gate."

"Gowan!"

A group of women was working its way to the exit. Behind them, Morna waved.

He felt like he could breathe again. If so many people hadn't been ahead of them, he would have gone back to Morna, grasped her hand, and run. Instead, Gowan inched his way forward and stole glances at Morna.

When they passed through the gate, Gowan swept Morna into his arms and swung her about. Then he held her close and pressed his cheek to hers. "Are you all right?"

She leaned away with a smile so bright, it had to be false. "I'm well! Why wouldn't I be? I'm with you! So tell me what happened to you!"

They shared stories of their two nights in the poorhouse, then Gowan stopped walking and turned to face Morna. "I'm sorry I put you through that."

Morna shook her head and said emphatically, "Dinnae be sorry."

Gowan looked away, tamping down his emotions.

"I'm not." She took his face in her hands and forced him to look at her. "I'm not sorry for any moment that comes from being together." Her eyes softened.

Gowan glanced about at people strolling in the crisp autumn air. "My love, I would kiss you right now, but we'd wind up being arrested for public indecency."

Morna grinned. "Och, no! At least not until we have a

proper meal." She laughed, but she suddenly gasped, and her shoulders sank. "I've been robbed, so I've no money for food. And you probably dinnae remember this, but I had no money to get my horse out of the stable. We'll need to find some sort of work."

With a secretive grin, Gowan sat on a bench and pulled off his boot. Morna watched him with a confused look on her face as he pulled out a small stack of papers.

Her eyes widened. "Those aren't... Are those..."

"Bank notes? Aye." Gowan smiled as he tucked one of the bills in his pocket and returned the rest to his boot. Standing, he offered his arm. "Shall we?"

"But there must be a dozen there, at least!"

He nodded. "A baker's dozen."

Her hand flew to her mouth. "Gowan, you didnae rob a bank, did you?"

He grinned and feigned offense. "How little you think of me. No, I earned it abroad." He shrugged. "There might be some card game winnings in there as well. But it's all ours."

"But how did you manage to keep it? When I was admitted to the poorhouse, they took all my clothes."

Gowan lifted an eyebrow. "I'm sorry I missed that." He smiled to see Morna turn away, blushing. "They dinnae search below the knee, and they let us keep our boots."

The next instant, her modest blush turned to annoyance. "If you had money, then why did you let them put us in the poorhouse?"

He leveled a look. "Lass, if they'd known we had money, do you think we'd still have it?"

"But they were constables!"

"Aye, and chances are they were honest, but that wasnae a wager I was willing to make."

Morna scratched her head. "Och. These tiny vermin. I'm itching all over." She cast a sharp look at Gowan. "I suppose I should thank you for these too."

"I'll make it up to you. We need to hide out for a sennight or so, until your father's guards give up and leave town. So why don't we pay to stable the horse while we're here, and we'll find a comfortable inn to hide out in. I'll order a hot bath, and you and your wee vermin can soak while I feed you fine food and drink."

Morna sighed. "That sounds lovely!"

SEVERAL BLOCKS past the bustling harbor, they happened upon a quaint little inn by the sea. Before they started up the walk to the door, Morna tugged on Gowan's arm. "We cannae check in with our own names."

"Oh, aye. If your father's men ask around, we'd best not make it easy for them."

Morna thought for a moment. "Smith? No. Too common and obvious."

"Brown? That's no better."

She leaned on his arm. "Let's think of something quickly. I'm so tired of walking. I just want to sit down."

Gowan's face lit up as he offered her his arm. "Well, Mrs. Walker, then let us go inquire about a room."

"Brilliant! The Walkers!" She slipped her arm into his, then Mr. and Mrs. Walker went up to the door.

An hour later, Morna sank into a hot bath while Gowan proved true to his word and fed her bread, cheese, and wine. Then he sat back and watched her with a mischievous grin. "You look lonely in that bath all alone." He peeled off his clothing and joined her.

When the bathwater grew cold, Gowan brought two towels he'd left warming by the fireplace. He dried off in haste then took his time drying Morna and led her by the hand to their bed. When he leaned over to kiss her, a wistful look clouded his face.

"What is it?"

"You would have had a fine wedding, worn a beautiful dress, and been surrounded by your family and friends, and I've taken that from you."

"Aye, a fine wedding with the wrong groom."

"You deserve more than to be wed by a blacksmith."

"Oh, aye, a saddler, at least."

When Morna saw Gowan's confusion, she said, "I noticed a sign at the stable. The saddler does weddings there."

Gowan did not look impressed.

Morna shrugged. "What does it matter who does it as long as we're married?"

"You'd be happy with that?"

"Aye, because you make me happy."

His eyes shone. "When we've been here a week and your father's men have given up and gone home, will you marry me?" For the first time since she'd met him, he looked almost lost.

"You know I will."

Gowan let out such a sigh of relief that Morna couldn't help but laugh. "What did you think I was doing here with you? Did you think I was dragging your drugged body around, sleeping in wynds on the ground, and knitting at the neighborhood poorhouse for my entertainment? It's all for you. And I'd do it all over again to be with you because I love you."

"Good. Because all I want is to love you for the rest of your life."

She kissed him, then he held her and kissed her and gave her his heart and his body all over again.

Chapter Twenty

On their seventh afternoon at the seaside inn, the elderly innkeeper's wife smiled as Gowan and Morna ventured outside. They had waited a week, confining themselves to their room except for moonlit walks along the shoreline late at night. Confident that her father's men had given up, they walked out into the sunlight.

"Och, it's so bright!" Morna laughed as she shielded her eyes.

"I'll guide you." Gowan put his arm about her waist and drew her closer.

Morna shoved her shoulder against him. "Oh, I ken where you're guiding me—straight back to bed."

He looked at her slyly. "I rather like it there."

She did a poor job of hiding her smile. "Well, I'm getting married today. So if you'd care to join me, you'd best set your mind on the task at hand."

After glancing about to make sure no one was near, he slid his hand upward from her waist. "Task at hand. Is that what you call it?"

Genuinely mortified that he would behave so in public, Morna swatted his hand away. That only drew laughter from Gowan, which she ignored. "I've a mind to marry you by proxy."

He wrinkled his face. "By what?"

"It means I'll marry you, but if you dinnae behave, I'll drag someone in off the street to stand in your place for the ceremony."

"Sorry, my love, but I'll not let that happen." He leaned closer. "The only reason I'm doing this is for the kiss at the end."

She took his arm. "Gowan?"

"Aye, lass?"

"Stop talking and walk." Her eyes shone as her lips spread into the smile she'd been suppressing.

Minutes later, they stood in a stable and were married by a saddler who looked and, when the wind shifted, smelled hungover. Halfway through the brief ceremony, Morna and Gowan looked at each other and nearly burst into laughter. As the poor saddler hastened to finish and ran away looking as though he were about to be sick, they turned to each other.

Morna said, "You may kiss the bride."

Before she'd finished the sentence, Gowan swept her into his arms and thoroughly kissed her. "Mrs. Dunbar."

Her eyes filled with stars. "Aye?"

"I like the sound of it. Mrs. Dunbar. My wife." His eyes might have stayed fixed on hers if the saddler had not returned with a paper to sign.

They walked outside, and Morna sighed.

"What is it, my love?"

She dismissed him with a shake of her head. "Och, it will just go to your head."

"Mrs. Dunbar, as your husband, I demand that you tell me."

She turned with a wide-eyed look that prompted a quick change in his demeanor. "I was just thinking of what an adventure it is to be with you. We've fled from ruffians, gotten arrested!" With a smile, she looked dreamily into the distance.

Gowan straightened his posture defensively. "For vagrancy. 'Tis not like I dragged you into a life of crime."

Morna smiled. "No, but you cannae deny life together has had its moments of excitement."

His face brightened. "Aye, which moments are those?"

She shut her eyes and shook her head. "Mr. Dunbar."

"Aye, missus?"

"Since we're making demands—"

"I was, not you."

With a slight smirk, Morna said, "Aye, so I noticed. But I have a demand of my own."

His eyebrows drew together in obvious dread.

She smiled and looked into his eyes. "There will be no more demanding between us."

Grinning, he said, "Aye, fair enough." He took her hand as they walked down the street. "I should have known when we met, and I first felt your knife at my neck, that life with you would be—"

"Perfect?"

"Aye, that's just what I was thinking."

IN THE LATE AFTERNOON, having been married and had a fine meal, they took their time strolling back to the inn.

Gowan had not stopped smiling since the wedding. "So let's see what we've decided. We'll have a large family with lots of wee ones running about."

Morna nodded. "Three."

"Or four?"

With a secretive smile, she said, "I could be convinced."

Gowan's eyes twinkled. "I look forward to that. And we'll all have beautifully hand-knitted mufflers and mittens."

Unruffled, she said, "Purchased from someone who knits beautifully."

"And we'll live off the land. I'll go hunting and fishing."

"With me."

"Aye, Mrs. Dunbar. I'd have it no other way."

When no one was about, Gowan leaned over and kissed her as if he'd never kissed her before. And Morna was sure she could grow old and still feel the same thrill every time his lips touched hers, and she breathed in his manly scent.

He moaned, "Mrs. Dunbar..." and shook his head and smiled as they continued on their way.

At their favorite spot to look out at the sea, they stopped, and Gowan took both of Morna's hands in his. "Mrs. Dunbar, do you ken what would make me even happier?"

"No, what?"

"Nothing." He grinned with that boyish grin that had first charmed her, then he looked out at the sea. "Other than the rest of our lives together."

"That sounds like a very long time." But as she turned to him, her playful smile faded, until only the light in her eyes remained.

He slid his palm down from her shoulders to her waist. "If you keep looking at me like that, I may sweep you up into my arms and run back to our room."

"I fear my weight would slow you down."

He carefully weighed his words. "Lass, you're as light as a feather, but I ken how you love vigorous outdoor activity, so I'll let you run on your own."

Morna regarded him with unbridled amusement. "Well done. Since you're so keen on vigorous activity..." She took off in a run and called back, "I'll race you to the gate!"

A minute later, Morna touched the gatepost just after Gowan then stood catching her breath. "'Tis not fair. These heavy skirts slow me down."

In apparent seriousness, Gowan nodded. "Then we'd best dispense with them."

"Gowan! You're incorrigible!"

He grinned and took her hand. "Aye, but you married me, so you cannae be rid of me now."

Laughing, they bounded into the inn but stopped short.

The innkeeper's wife stood blocking their way up the stairs with her arms folded and lips pursed in full disapproval. "You have a visitor... Mr. and Mrs. Walker. Humph! I run a respectable establishment here."

Gowan and Morna both turned to look through the open door to the parlor.

For a moment, Morna froze, then softly she said, "Mr. Huntly!"

Gowan said nothing, but Morna felt him grow tense and pull up taller as he stood beside her.

Huntly lowered his chin. "Miss Innes—or should I say Mrs. Walker. He cast a chilling glare toward Gowan.

Morna said, "How did you ken we were here?"

Huntly cleared his throat. "I didnae. I'm in Aberdeen every sennight, as I believe I mentioned... while we were... courting." His eyebrows drew together.

Morna wasn't sure whether his discomfort was from anger or pain. Either one filled her with guilt.

Continuing, Huntly said, "I was riding in my carriage when I happened to see you out walking today. So I got out and worked my way down the road, making inquiries at each inn and boarding house until I arrived here."

Gowan drew in a breath. "Morna and I are now married. I'm sorry for... any disappointment it causes."

Huntly blurted out with an unexpected release of anger, "I'm not here for myself. Your father is a longtime friend of mine. And he's ill."

A small cry came from Morna's throat. "Ill?"

Huntly nodded. "Quite ill. If you care—"

Morna cried, "Of course I care! He's my father."

Huntly cleared his throat again, as if doing so would keep his emotions in check. "As I was saying, if you care to see him before... You should go to him now."

Morna exchanged glances with Gowan then turned back to Huntly. "Of course."

Huntly gave a nod and directed his next words solely

to Morna. "I've a carriage outside. If you'd like, I can take you."

"That willnae be necessary," Gowan said firmly.

"As you wish. Good day, then." Huntly nodded and left.

Chapter Twenty-One

Gowan and Morna arrived at Innes House in the middle of the night. Sionn woke up and sleepily took care of their horse. Morna started toward the house, but Gowan held onto her hand. "I'll stay here. I'm sure Sionn has some hay he could spare for me to sleep on."

"You will not!"

He calmly looked at her and waited for her to think it through. "It won't do to upset your father when he's ill. I'll stay out here. He need not know I'm on the grounds."

Morna said, "You are my husband. I'll not hide you in a horse stall."

Gowan did not look convinced.

"You will stay in my room. I'll not hide you away, but I'll not upset him, either. We'll wait for the right time to tell him." When that would be, she had no idea.

Putting his hands on her shoulders, Gowan said, "As you wish."

He enveloped her in his arms but then caught sight of

young Sionn, who was watching with interest. Gowan's mouth turned up at the corner. "We'd best go."

After getting settled in her room, Morna instructed the butler to make sure no one mentioned Gowan's presence to her father. With that done, Morna rushed to her father's room. A nurse answered the door and seemed keen on keeping Morna out.

Morna said, "I'm his daughter."

The nurse held her ground. "He needs his rest."

A weak voice came from inside. "Morna?"

"Father, I'm here."

With a disapproving frown, the nurse stepped aside. Morna rushed to her father and pulled a chair close to his bed. She sat down and took hold of his hand. He looked weak and, for the first time, old.

He looked up at her. "Morna."

"Father, I'm here. Get some sleep. I'll be here when you wake."

His hand tightened weakly about hers. "You broke my heart."

And you broke mine. Her throat tightened. "I'm sorry. We'll talk later. Right now, you need to rest. I love you." She squeezed his hand and sat back while he drifted to sleep.

THE NEXT MORNING, when the doctor left Malcolm's room, Morna was waiting. They went down to the parlor to talk in private.

"He's stable."

Her face brightened.

"For now."

Morna forced herself to face the truth. "He said I broke his heart. I brought this on."

"Och no, lass. Dinnae take on that burden. His heart is weak. He's known for some time he was ill."

Morna's first impulse was to tell him he was wrong, but deep down, she knew better. "I had no idea."

"Aye, well, that's Malcolm, is it not? Invincible to the end."

His words struck a hard blow. To the end. She was not ready for that. "Is there nothing I can do?"

"Nothing you're not already doing."

Morna thanked him and walked with him to the door. Then she went to her room to find Gowan, but he was not there. One of the servants said she'd seen him earlier on his way to the stables.

She nodded then went to sit with her father. He slept for most of the morning, but his breathing was troubled. The sun shone through a gap in the curtains. Morna rose to go open them, and when she returned to her father's bedside, he woke and put his hand on hers. He looked up with love in his eyes, then his eyes widened. He took in a breath, tried to sit up, and gulped in more air, then he lay down and didn't breathe again.

Morna knew he was gone, but she waited. He'd only just left. He might breathe again. She knew better, but she could not let go.

The nurse came in, and Morna looked up. From the nurse's expression, Morna could see that she knew he was gone, though she went to him and checked to make sure.

Morna quietly got up and left.

"SIONN, PLEASE SADDLE MY HORSE."

"Aye, miss." He looked up at her, concerned, as she paced.

"Thank you."

A few minutes later, she rode through the gates. Gowan was not in her room, so he must have gone out for a ride. They'd find each other later. Right now, Morna just needed to ride, feel the wind, and put distance between her and sorrow.

The mountains loomed large, protecting the glen that cut through them. The sun tried to break through the dense clouds in spots, but the sky left more shadows than light on the land. Not even the grand Innes House was immune to Scotland's tempestuous skies.

Only love could have managed to draw her away from this place. No matter how long she was gone, something deep in her restless soul would always call her back to these hills. For all of her life, she'd roamed freely yet always remaining within its bounds. This was her home, as it had been for generations of her family before her. But her father, for all of his faults, had been the core of the home. Now he was gone, but, like his family before him, he'd returned to the land that had anchored them there. She stood astride her horse and looked out at the majestic countryside that was Scotland, her home, and she felt small yet grounded in its grandeur.

With no destination in mind, she wandered until she came to the pool where she'd first met Gowan. She stood deep in thought as her horse drank from the stream that fed into the pool. Her father had known he was ill. Perhaps it had not been Huntly who was so eager for the marriage but her father, instead. He was the one who had been so keen to marry her off. In his own way, he wanted to take care of her.

The sound of hoofbeats came closer, and Gowan approached. "I thought I might find you here." He dismounted and joined Morna. "I went back to the house, and Sionn said you'd gone riding."

"I thought if I rode hard enough along the same paths Robert and I used to ride, it might feel like it used to." She swallowed. "But you cannae bring it back, can you? Those days and those people are gone."

Gowan gripped her shoulder. "Robert loved you so deeply. I wonder if he didn't somehow have a sense, when he sent me to you, that I'd love you."

She attempted a smile. "I think he sent you to me out of fear that no one else would love me."

His eyes crinkled at the corners. "And no one will, for I'll not let them."

They smiled, but Morna's grief would not leave her for long. "Robert was his favorite. Had he been able to choose which child to lose, he would not have picked Robert."

Gowan slipped his hand about hers.

"Father and I were always at odds. If I'd let him, he would have ignored me. But in the end, I was hard to ignore."

"Morna, what your father did, both to me and to you, was done out of love for you."

"I wonder how many wrongs are done in the name of love."

He put his arm about her and cradled her head on his shoulder. "No one knows because they are followed by forgiveness, and that is not counted. Just remember that your father loved you. Hold that in your heart."

Chapter Twenty-Two

Morna buried her father and mourned along with the dozens who'd known him and come from miles around to express their condolences. Before leaving, William Huntly found Morna in a rare moment alone.

"My condolences. I wish you well."

"Thank you, Mr. Huntly."

He hesitated. "When I last visited Malcolm, he asked me to write a letter for him, which I did. He made me promise not to give it to you until now." Huntly handed the letter to Morna and left.

Later, as the last of the visitors rode away, Gowan stood beside Morna in the uncanny quiet of Innes House.

Morna said, "I want to go for a ride." She turned and looked up at him. "Will you join me?"

The morning rain had let up, and one ribbon of sun found its way through the clouds to the valley. Morna led the way to the top of the hill overlooking Innes House. There, they stopped and gazed down. A long silence passed.

Morna quietly said, "I've come here so many times over the years, most often with Robert. As children, we played. As we grew older, we used to think about how it would be when we were grown. We were up here, sitting on the grass over there, when he told me he was in love with Briana. He was so happy."

She gave a soft, despairing sigh. "Why don't we know in those moments that they're to be treasured?"

Gowan said nothing, but the faraway look in his eyes told her he was thinking of moments in his own life.

She continued, "Some of us survive—not because we are stronger but because that's how things happen sometimes. So much of it is chance. We are merely the ones left to mourn." She pulled the letter that Huntly had given her from her pocket. "Huntly gave this to me."

A flash of anger came over him. "What the devil does he think he's doing?"

"No, it's from my father. He asked Huntly to write his words down." Morna turned the letter over in her hands and looked down at Innes House. Then she handed the letter to Gowan to read.

MY DEAR MORNA,

WHEN YOUR MOTHER DIED, I didn't know what to do with you. I thought you might grow to be like her, but you have a mind of your own.

When I fell ill, I wanted to be sure you'd be taken care

of. *I could think of no finer man for that job than William Huntly. But you have a heart of your own.*

I've learned something from you. You and Gowan Dunbar will have your own children, so I will pass on to you this one lesson, which I have learned the hard way. You will do what you think is right, but your children will confound you in spite of it all.

There's only one thing you need do, and it's love. I wish I'd done it better, but know that I loved you.

ALWAYS,

FATHER

Chapter Twenty-Three

Seven Years Later

Morna glanced into the mirror then looked closer. "Och, who are you?" She started to tuck bits of hair back into place, then she blotted her glistening face with her sleeve. "'Tis no use." She gave up and answered the door.

"Come in, Doctor. He's in here." She led him back to the kitchen, where a child sat at the large wooden table, looking nonplussed.

With a smile, the doctor said, "Young Master Dunbar. How are you today?"

When the boy said nothing, the doctor gave Morna a quizzical look.

She folded her arms and frowned. "It's his ear. Hamish has stuffed woolen yarn into his ear, and it's in too far. I cannae get it out."

The doctor's mouth turned up at the corner as he bent down to examine the boy.

A frazzled Morna said, "He seems to just wait until Gowan is gone, then he does things like this."

"I seem to recall you and your brother getting into your own mischief."

"Och, you must be thinking of someone else!" She cast an urgent, conspiratorial look at her son and gave her head a small shake.

With a smile, the doctor examined the boy's ear.

A cry rang out from above.

"Please excuse me, Doctor." She took off at a run toward the stairs.

Down marched her six-year-old daughter, doll in hand.

"Marjory! Are you all right?"

She thrust the doll toward her mother. "Look what he's done!"

The doll's hair was cut off to ragged bits sticking out in all directions. Morna exhaled, relieved. From the sound of the cry, she'd expected the worst—possibly blood.

"I hate him!" Then a sly look came into her daughter's eyes, and she said nonchalantly, "Hamish's lead soldiers accidentally fell into the fire. They might be a wee bit melted."

Morna frowned. "Marjory, really! Go to your room. We'll talk about this later."

Gowan walked in the door, just returned from a business trip to Aberdeen. "There they are! My lovely lassies!"

Two angry females turned, glaring.

Morna turned back to her daughter. "Go on." One stern glance upward sent the child up the stairs to her room.

Morna went down the remaining few steps to the floor. "Come with me."

Gowan braced himself then followed.

They arrived just in time to find the doctor pulling an inches-long strand of yarn out of Hamish's ear. "There we are." The doctor held out the tweezers with dangling yarn as if it were a trophy. "All better now."

Morna frowned at her son. "Up you go to your room. We'll be up in a minute." When he hesitated, she pointed.

After thanking the doctor, they both walked him to the door. Gowan closed the door, and Morna collapsed against it.

"The governess went home to care for her sick mother. And those children! They're so... difficult!"

Gowan turned her to face him and grinned. "Aye, they take after you."

Her eyes widened. "Oh, you can laugh. I'm half mad. I dinnae ken what to do with them."

He drew her into an embrace. "Someone once said..."

Morna sighed. "Love them."

Gowan grinned and shrugged. "That's what I do when you get difficult. I love you."

Her eyes widened again, and she took in a breath, but he kissed her until she forgot what she'd wanted to say, what the children had done, and nearly everything else.

Then, arm in arm, they walked up the stairs.

Thank You!

Thank you for reading! If you enjoyed this book, please consider leaving a review or a rating. Your feedback on bookstore, Goodreads, and Bookbub websites helps other readers discover books they'll enjoy.

Thank You!

Thank you for reading! If you enjoyed this book, please consider leaving a review or a rating on Amazon or your favorite bookstore. Your feedback helps other readers discover my work.

Book News

Sign up for the J.L. Jarvis Journal for exclusive benefits, including free books, special offers, exclusive content, and updates on new releases: news.jljarvis.com

Book News

Sign up for the J.L. Jarvis Journal for exclusive benefits, including free books, special offers, exclusive content, and updates on new releases: news.jljarvis.com

Also by J.L. Jarvis

Waterfront Summers

(Can be read in any order)

The Cottage at Peregrine Cove

The House on Serenity Lake

Moonlight on Mariner's Bluff

Drake & Wilde Mysteries

(Reading Order)

1 Love in the Time of Pumpkins

2 Secrets in the Hollow

3 Shadow of the Horseman

Standalones

(Can be read in any order)

A Christmas Eve Stop

Christmas by Lamplight

A Kiss in the Rain

App-ily Ever After

Once Upon a Winter

The Red Rose

Highland Vow

Short Stories

(Can be read in any order)

Seasons of Love: A Short Story Collection

The Eleventh-Hour Pact

A Christmas Yarn

The Farmer and the Belle

Work-Crush Balance

Cedar Creek

(Can be read in any order)

Christmas at Cedar Creek

Snowstorm at Cedar Creek

Sunlight on Cedar Creek

Pine Harbor

1 Allison's Pine Harbor Summer

2 Evelyn's Pine Harbor Autumn

3 Lydia's Pine Harbor Christmas

Holiday House

(Can be read in any order)

The Christmas Cabin

The Winter Lodge

The Lighthouse

The Christmas Castle

The Beach House

The Christmas Tree Inn

The Holiday Hideaway

Highland Passage

For more information, visit jljarvis.com.

Get monthly book news at news.jljarvis.com.

About the Author

J.L. Jarvis is a left-handed former opera singer/teacher/lawyer who writes books. She now lives and writes on a mountaintop in upstate New York.

jljarvis.com

Acknowledgments

Editing by Red Adept Editing
redadeptediting.com